THE BARONS

**Four brothers:
bonded by their inheritance, battling for love!**

Jonas Baron is approaching his eighty-fifth
birthday. He has ruled Espada, his sprawling
estate in Texas hill country, for more than
forty years, but now he admits it's time he
chose an heir.

Jonas has three sons—Gage, Travis and Slade,
all ruggedly handsome and each with a successful
business empire of his own; none wishes to give
up the life he's fought for to take over Espada.
Jonas also has a stepdaughter; beautiful and
spirited, Caitlin loves the land as much as he
does, but she's not of the Baron blood.

So who will receive Baron's bequest? In this,
the fourth book in THE BARONS series, a
new character becomes a contender—
mysterious stranger Tyler Kincaid....

Be sure to look out next for
more fabulous stories about the Baron family
in months to come.

SANDRA MARTON

The Taming of Tyler Kincaid

THE BARONS

HARLEQUIN®

TORONTO • NEW YORK • LONDON
AMSTERDAM • PARIS • SYDNEY • HAMBURG
STOCKHOLM • ATHENS • TOKYO • MILAN • MADRID
PRAGUE • WARSAW • BUDAPEST • AUCKLAND

ISBN 0-373-12081-8

THE TAMING OF TYLER KINCAID

First North American Publication 2000.

This edition published by arrangement with Harlequin Books S.A.

® and TM are trademarks of the publisher. Trademarks indicated with
® are registered in the United States Patent and Trademark Office, the
Canadian Trade Marks Office and in other countries.

Visit us at www.romance.net

Printed in U.S.A.

CHAPTER ONE

IT WAS Tyler Kincaid's birthday, and he had the feeling his present was waiting in his bed.

Atlanta sweltered under the oppressive heat of the July evening, but he didn't mind. He'd lived in the South all his life and he liked the warm days and hot, sultry nights. He had nothing against finding a woman in his bed, either, especially a beautiful blonde like Adrianna. Under normal circumstances, a man would have to be crazy to object to that.

Tyler frowned as he slowed his Porsche outside the wrought-iron gates that guarded his hilltop estate.

But these weren't normal circumstances.

If he was right and Adrianna was waiting for him complete with champagne, caviar and flowers, she'd entered his home uninvited. There'd been times he'd asked his mistress to spend the night, but he'd never given her or any woman access to his life—or to the security codes that unlocked the gates and the massive front door to his home.

And he damned well hadn't made any plans to celebrate his birthday.

July 18 was just another day in the year, as far as he was concerned. He never so much as circled the day on his calendar. If there was anything special about the date it was because he'd realized, just this morning, that it was time to tell Adrianna their relationship was over.

The gates swung shut behind him. Ahead, a narrow road lined with magnolia trees led toward the big white house he'd bought on the same day he'd taken his company's stock public eight years ago. By day's end, Tyler had gone from being poor white trash to being a millionaire several times over. "An outstanding citizen," the *Atlanta Journal* had called him. Tyler had saved the article, kept it in a scrapbook right next

5

to the clipping dated ten years before that, when the same newspaper had said he was "an example of Atlanta's lost youth."

There was a nice irony there but that wasn't why he'd kept both articles. He'd kept them, rather, as a reminder of how a man's life could change with a couple of orbits of the planet around the sun.

"You're a true cynic, Tyler," his attorney had once said with a sigh of mild despair, but Tyler figured there wasn't anything wrong with acknowledging that nothing in this world was ever quite what it seemed.

Especially a relationship with a woman.

He sighed, shut off the engine and looked at the house. It seemed deserted, except for the lights shining at some of the windows, but he knew those came on automatically, at dusk. They were part of his security system. His impenetrable security system, according to the outfit that had installed it.

"Impenetrable, my butt," Tyler muttered.

To thieves, maybe, but not to the machinations of a determined, blue-eyed blonde.

There was no sign of her, no little green Mercedes convertible parked in the driveway. He'd expected that. Adrianna was bright as well as beautiful. His women always scored high, on brains as well as looks. She'd have found a place to tuck the car away where he wouldn't see it.

How else could she hope to surprise him?

Tyler's jaw tightened. He sat back in the leather bucket seat and spread his hands along the steering wheel.

The thing of it was, he didn't like surprises, certainly not ones that involved his birthday, and definitely not when the surprise suggested a woman, even a beautiful, eminently desirable woman, was getting ideas about changing the status quo.

He'd made himself clear, at the start of their affair. People change, he'd told her. Their goals change, their needs change. Adrianna had smiled, interrupted, and said she understood.

"Darling, I promise you," she'd murmured, "I'm not the least bit interested in fairy tales that end with forever-after."

She wasn't. That was one of the things he admired about her. She lived an independent life, a Southern belle in looks and background but a modern woman when it came to making her way in the world.

He'd made it clear he liked his privacy, too—meaning he wanted none of her makeup left in his bathroom, nor would he leave his shaving things in hers. There'd be no mutual exchange of house keys or security codes—she'd laughed when he'd said that, in that husky voice that had, in those first weeks, made his blood hum.

"Darling, you're just the sort of man that turns me on. A gorgeous rogue, lover, that's what you are. Why would a woman be foolish enough to want to tame you?"

Fidelity, for as long as the affair lasted, was all they'd committed to. That was all Tyler was still committed to...but, evidently, somewhere along the way, Adrianna had changed her mind.

Tyler opened the door of the Porsche and stepped out. Cicadas sang in the trees; the heavy scent of jasmine enveloped him. He looked up at the house, at his bedroom windows, and wondered if she were watching him through the silky curtains.

He imagined her, warm and naked and flushed from the shower. Or wearing the body-skimming black silk nightgown he'd given her. He had to admit, the sexual fantasy was a turn-on.

A tentative smile tugged at the corner of his mouth. Okay, so she'd taken things a bit far but maybe he was doing the same thing. So what if she'd watched him enter the security codes and memorized them? That had to be the way she'd gotten in. And she'd probably gone through his wallet when he was asleep, checked his driver's license to learn his birthday.

Was that so terrible?

It wasn't. Not really. He could deal with it, he told himself as he climbed the steps to the veranda. Dealing with things was what he did.

Tyler could feel the tension easing inside him, now that he

was willing to admit he'd overreacted. Okay. He'd open the door, step inside the marble foyer. Undo his tie, take off his jacket, dump his briefcase on the table. Then he'd go up to his bedroom, open the door, find Adrianna waiting for him in a room filled with roses, a flute of champagne in her hand and a silver bowl heaped with Beluga caviar beside the bed.

"Surprise, darling," she'd purr, and he'd smile and pretend it really was a surprise, that he hadn't expected her to be there, that his caterer hadn't spilled the secret.

Actually it had been the caterer's new, eager-to-please assistant who'd phoned him.

"Mr. Kincaid," she'd said, "this is Susan. At Le Bon Appetit? I'm calling about that order you placed for delivery to your home this evening."

Tyler, who'd been paying most of his attention to the Dow-Jones numbers racing across the screen of his computer, had frowned.

"What?"

"I've checked our records, sir, and I see that you always order Krug. I just wanted to be certain you actually wanted Dom Pérignon this time."

"No. I mean, there's been a mistake. I did not—"

"Ah. Well, sir, that's what I thought. That there'd been a mistake, you know? The clerk must have gotten the order wrong."

"No," Tyler said, "the clerk did not—"

"That's kind of you, Mr. Kincaid, "suggesting it was Ms. Kirby who made the error, but—"

Tyler had gone very still. "Adrianna Kirby ordered champagne to be delivered to my home?"

"And Beluga caviar, sir. And roses. And a cake. Oh, I hope that cake isn't for you, sir. I'd hate to think I gave away a surprise."

Tyler had closed his eyes. "No," he'd said, "actually, you've been—you've been quite helpful."

And, just like that, it had all fallen into place, the little signals he'd managed to ignore the past couple of weeks.

"Here's a key to my apartment, Tyler," Adrianna had said,

folding his hand around the bit of metal, smiling when he'd frowned. "Oh, get that look off your face, darling. You don't have to reciprocate. It's just in case I'm in the bath or something, when you come by."

And there was the way she'd taken to dropping by his office without calling first. She was in the neighborhood, she'd say, and wouldn't lunch be lovely? The earrings she'd "forgotten" in his bathroom. Yes, and those soft little sighs of disappointment, whenever he rose from her bed and started to dress.

"You really could stay the night, darling," she'd purr, even though she knew he never would.

"Hell," Tyler muttered.

"Idiot" was too kind a word to describe him. And now, there was Adrianna, waiting in his bedroom to celebrate an occasion that was common to every creature on the planet, waiting for him with flowers and champagne and a handful of dreams he had no intention of sharing.

Okay. Okay, he'd do the right thing, act surprised, even pleased. And then, in a few days, in a week, he'd gently put an end to things.

He punched in the code. The door swung open. Lights blazed on, and a hundred voices shouted, "Surprise!"

Tyler blinked in astonishment, took a quick step back and stared at the blur of laughing faces.

"Darling," Adrianna shrieked, and flew toward him in a shimmering cloud of fuchsia silk, golden hair and Chanel.

"Happy thirty-fifth birthday, darling." She looked up at him and smiled. "Surprised?"

His face felt stiff. "Yes," he said. "Very surprised."

Adrianna laughed and looped her arm through his. "Just look at his face," she said to the crowd around them. "Tyler, dearest, I know exactly what you're thinking."

Everybody laughed, everybody but Tyler, who was working at keeping his smile locked into place.

"I doubt it," he said.

Adrianna tossed her head so that her hair flowed over her bare shoulders.

"You're wondering how I managed all this. The invitations.

The food, the champagne, the flowers. The band.'' As if on cue, music wafted down from the balcony that overlooked the great room. She looped her arms around his neck and began to move in time with it. Tyler forced himself to hang on to the smile and to move with her. "And the most difficult part, darling. Slipping your wallet from your pocket and going through it, to learn your actual birthday after you let slip that the big Three-Five was coming up.''

"Did I?'' he said, wondering how, and when, and why he'd been so loose-lipped.

"At that dinner for the mayor last month, remember? Someone at our table was moaning about turning forty, and you grinned and said wasn't it a pity he was such an old fogy, that you were only just approaching—''

All Tyler's good intentions fled. "I wish you hadn't done this, Adrianna.''

His mistress laughed softly. "You're just annoyed that I peeked over your shoulder while you entered those codes.''

"Yes. And that you went through my wallet. And that you arranged this party.''

"Don't you like surprises, darling?''

"No,'' he said coldly, "I do not.''

"Well, then, next time, you can help me plan your party.'' Adrianna smiled coyly. "We could even make it a special occasion, Tyler. After all, we'll have been together more than a year by then.''

Tyler didn't answer. He took her hand in his, put his other arm around her waist and whirled her in a head-spinning circle while he wondered just how long it would take for the night to end.

An eternity, that was how long. That was how long it seemed, anyway.

The last guests finally left, the last catering van departed. The house was silent, the big, expensively decorated rooms were empty, now filled only with the lingering traces of perfume and roses.

"I'll take you home,'' Tyler had said to Adrianna. He'd

known his voice was expressionless, his eyes cold, but he'd done the best he could and now it was time to deal with reality.

Either Adrianna hadn't recognized that, or she'd pretended not to.

"Let me get my things," she'd replied, and vanished up the stairs.

He'd waited and waited, pacing the length of the foyer, telling himself to control his temper, that he could, at least, end this thing without a scene. After five or ten minutes, he'd scowled and gone upstairs.

Adrianna was in the shower. He could hear the water running in the bathroom.

Tyler had flung an oath into the darkened bedroom, jammed his hands into the pockets of his trousers and settled in to wait.

Now he stood at the window, staring out at the inky darkness, the façade he'd maintained the past few hours crumbling more with each passing minute. All evening he'd smiled, he'd chatted, he'd shaken hands with the men and kissed the women's cheeks when his guests had offered their birthday congratulations.

He puffed out his breath, watched it fog the glass. How generous would they have been with their good wishes, their handshakes, their kisses, if they knew the truth, he wondered. If the front door had opened and the boy he'd once been had come strolling across the marble floor, his defiant expression just daring anybody to try to throw him out.

The thought was so preposterous it almost made him laugh.

"Damned fine party, Kincaid," the mayor had said, clapping him on the shoulder. "Not every man gets to celebrate his birthday in such style."

My birthday, Tyler thought. His mouth twisted. Who in hell knew if this was his birthday or not? The truth was, he might have come into this world yesterday, or maybe even the day before that. Babies that were dumped on hospital doorsteps didn't come complete with birth certificates.

The Brightons, who'd raised him, had told him all about it. They told him how he'd been found and given to them. They'd told him, too, that nobody was sure exactly what day he'd

been born, but that the authorities figured he'd been somewhere between one and three days old, when he was found.

When he was really little, he just hadn't understood it.

"Everybody has a real birthday," he'd said, and the
Brightons would say yes, that was true. And he had one. Those
same anonymous authorities had decided on July 18.

"But who was my mommy?" he'd ask. "And my daddy?"

Myra and James Brighton would look at each other, then at
him. "We're your parents," one of them would say.

But they weren't. Oh, they were kind to him. Or perhaps it
was more accurate to say they didn't mistreat him—but he
knew they never loved him. He saw how it was, with other
kids. How a father smoothed a hand over a son's hair, how a
mother pulled her boy close and kissed him.

Tyler's life wasn't like that. Nobody touched him, or kissed
him. Nobody hugged him when his grades were good or even
got angry when they weren't.

And his name. Tyler's mouth thinned with the pain of the
memory. John Smith, for God's sake. John Smith. How could
a boy grow up with a name like that?

He'd wanted to change it but the Brightons said he couldn't.

"It's your name, John," James Brighton said.

So it was. And he lived with it. With all of it. By the time
he was ten, he'd stopped asking questions that never were
answered. What was the point? The Brightons never adopted
him, never gave him their name—and then, in one fatal moment, his entire life changed. The three of them were on a
Sunday outing when a truck hit their car.

Tyler wasn't so much as scratched. He stood by the side of
the road, a policeman's big hand on his shoulder, watching
without a trace of expression on his face as his foster parents'
bodies were removed from the wreck and taken away.

"The kid's in shock," he heard the cop tell the social
worker who came for him and maybe he was. But the reality
was that deep down, he couldn't mourn people he'd never
known.

The state took him in. He was sent to live in a place with

lots of other boys like him, kids nobody gave a damn about, kids with no future—

But even they had real names.

He took a lot of crap over his.

"John Smith," the kids said with sneers. "Who're you kidding? Nobody's named John Smith."

They were right, and Tyler knew it. On the day he turned sixteen—the day his bogus birth certificate said he turned sixteen—he took his first name from a chapter in his American history textbook and his second from a character in a TV movie.

The kids laughed and sneered even harder.

"Nobody names himself," they said.

"I do," Tyler had replied, and when they went on laughing, he bloodied some noses, beat one kid to his knees. No one ever laughed again.

From then on, Tyler Kincaid was who he was. It was Tyler Kincaid who danced on the edge of the juvenile justice system, not John Smith. Tyler Kincaid who finally got caught joyriding in a car he'd "borrowed" from a mall, Tyler Kincaid who lucked out—though he sure hadn't thought so, at the time—and got sentenced to eight months at a place called Boys Ranch, where he learned something about horses and maybe even about himself.

At eighteen, he left the Ranch and enlisted in the Marines.

When he got out, he made the name legal, took a job at a working ranch, found he had a talent not just for horses but for understanding the relationship between capital investment and land. After that, he never thought about John Smith again—except once a year, maybe, when the day that was supposed to be the day of his birth rolled around. Tyler had learned to accept the date but he sure as hell didn't have to celebrate it. What was there to celebrate on a birthday that might not be your own, a birthday that marked the time your mother, maybe your old man, too, had dumped you on a doorstep like a sack of garbage rather than acknowledge your existence?

"Nothing," Tyler muttered, and reached for the half-empty

champagne bottle he'd gone downstairs and snagged. "Not one damned thing."

"Oh, dear."

He swung around. The bathroom door was open; Adrianna stood limned by light in the opening. He had to admit, she was magnificent. All that long golden hair, the black silk nightgown barely containing her breasts and clinging to her body, touching her the way his hands would…if he let himself touch her. She stood with one long, shapely leg thrust out through the thigh-high slit in the skirt of the gown, her high-arched foot encased in a black silk slipper with a heel so high it made his blood pressure soar.

"Talking to yourself, darling?" she whispered.

She came toward him, her walk slow, her hips swinging. The scent of Chanel drifted to his nostrils; he knew from experience that she'd touched it to all her pulse points, and to the soft skin of her thighs.

Take her, his blood sang, bury yourself in her…but his brain reminded him, coldly, that taking her now would only delay the inevitable. Despite everything she'd done, she deserved better than that.

"Adrianna." He cleared his throat, walked to the nightstand where she'd left her flute of champagne, picked it up and offered it to her. "We have to talk."

"Talk?" She smiled, took a sip of the wine and eyed him over the delicate rim of the glass. "Seems to me we can do better than that, darling. Here I am, all ready for bed, and you're still standing there in your suit." She put down her glass. "I'll help you, shall I?" Her hands went to his tie, to the first button on his shirt. "Let's get you out of this and—"

"No." Tyler caught hold of her wrists, drew down her hands. "Dammit, listen to me."

"You're hurting me, Tyler."

He looked at his hands, saw them crushing her delicate bones. "I'm sorry," he said stiffly, and let go of her. "Adrianna. About tonight—"

"The party."

"Yes. Right. The party." Only minutes ago, he'd intended

to end things between them by telling her she'd had no right to make the damned party, to invade his space, to presume things about their relationship that weren't valid, but she was looking up at him, wide-eyed, her mouth just starting to tremble. Instead of anger, he felt a quick, almost overwhelming despair. "I know that you must have gone to a lot of trouble, arranging it…"

"And you wish I hadn't."

"Yes. I wish you hadn't."

"I don't understand." Tears rose in her eyes, threatened to spill down her cheeks. "I only wanted to make you happy, darling."

"I know. But—" But what? Could a man really be angry at a woman for caring about him enough to want to give him a surprise party? "But," he said gently, "I never celebrate my birthday, Adrianna."

"That's just plain silly."

"It's fact."

"Oh, pooh." The tears that had threatened vanished in an instant. She smiled and put her palms flat against his chest. "We'll change all that."

"No." He caught her hands again, this time being careful not to apply any pressure. "No, we won't."

"Of course we will. Next year—"

"There isn't going to be a next year, Adrianna." He let go of her, ran his fingers through his dark hair. "Look, I'm trying my damnedest not to hurt your feelings, but—"

"My feelings? *My* feelings? Dammit, Tyler!" Her voice rose and he looked at her in surprise. He'd never heard her speak so stridently before. "Don't you dare patronize me. You don't give a rat's tail about my feelings." She lifted her hand, poked it, hard, into his chest. "You're just angry because I got tired of waiting for you to move our relationship on to the next phase."

Tyler's green eyes grew cool. "There is no next phase, Adrianna."

"Of course there is. All this nonsense, not letting me leave some of my things here, not ever spending the whole night at my place..." Her chin rose. "Acting as if letting me know those silly gate and door codes would violate national security."

His gaze went from cool to frigid. "I told you, right up-front, how things were going to be."

"No commitment. No forever-after."

"The no forever-after was your contribution."

"Maybe so. That was the way I felt, at the time—but I changed my mind."

"That's not my fault, baby," Tyler snapped. "I kept my end of the deal."

"And you're known for that, aren't you? For always keeping your end of the deal. Cool-headed Tyler Kincaid, never undermined by sentiment, in business or in his dealings with women."

Tyler puffed out a breath in exasperation. "Look, there's no point to this. I don't want to quarrel with you—"

"No. You just want to tell me I overstepped my bounds, that I had no right to waltz into your house, into your life."

"Dammit!" Tyler threaded his hand through his hair again. "Look, if I'd wanted a birthday party, I'd have thrown one for myself."

Adrianna rolled her eyes. "Good God, what a sin! Arranging a party—"

"Don't you get it? I didn't want a party."

"A party to which I invited a bunch of your friends—"

"They're not my friends."

"Of course they are!"

"They're people I know, that's all. They only bother with me because of what I can give them."

"Which is precious little, Tyler."

Tyler's mouth thinned. "What in hell is that supposed to mean?"

Adrianna swung away from him and stalked into the bathroom. "That magazine article the other week called you 'brilliant.' Figure it out for yourself."

He strode after her, watched as she stripped off the gown, pulled a T-shirt and jeans from her nightcase and put them on.

"I've set up deals for half the men who were here tonight," he growled, "and the other half wishes I would. You think that's giving them precious little, huh?"

"Is that what you think people want from you? Deals? Money? Power?"

Tyler stared at his mistress. She was fully dressed now, still wearing those high heels. Now, strangely, they struck him not as sexy but sad.

"Look," he said, struggling to sound calm, "it's late. We're both tired. I think it's best if I drive you home."

"I'm perfectly capable of driving myself home, thank you."

She was, and he knew it. Tyler shrugged his shoulders, folded his arms and leaned against the wall.

"Suit yourself."

"I intend to." Adrianna shot him a glittering smile. "It would never have worked, Tyler. I guess I always knew that, in my heart. After a while, whenever I looked at you, I'd see the look in your eyes that says 'Keep Out,' and it would have killed me."

Her words drained the anger from him.

"It isn't you," he said softly. "Despite anything I said, it isn't you."

"Sometimes…" She drew a deep breath. "Sometimes, I wonder if there's anybody inside you, Tyler. If you feel things, like the rest of us."

"Adrianna…"

"The thing is…" she said, with a little laugh. "The thing is, I fell in love with you. And I know you could never fall in love with me."

He thought of lying to her, of softening the blow, but he knew, too, that the one thing he could give her now was the truth. He reached out, tucked a strand of golden hair behind her ear.

"No," he said gently, "I couldn't. I wish it were different. I really wish—"

Adrianna put her hand lightly over his mouth. "Don't lie to either of us, Tyler. That isn't your wish. We both know

that I'm not the woman for you. I'm not the one you're looking for.''

Tyler gave a mocking laugh. "I'm not looking for a woman.
Not now, not ever. "

"Everyone's looking for someone, whether they know it or
not."

"You're wrong."

Adrianna smiled gently, rose on her toes and pressed a light
kiss to his mouth.

"Goodbye, darling," she whispered.

Tyler watched her walk from the room. He sank down on
the edge of the bed, listened to the distant *click- click* of those
ridiculous high heels fading, then to the even more distant
sound of her car. At last, he stood and walked slowly to the
window.

The moon was setting, dipping into the branches of the old
oak just outside his bedroom.

There was nobody inside him, Adrianna had said, but she
was wrong. Tyler smiled bitterly. The boy named John Smith
was still there, whether he liked it or not. There was an emptiness in his heart, a yearning sometimes that he couldn't put
a name to or get rid of by burying himself in his work, or
even by pounding his gloved fists against the body bag at his
gym.

She was wrong about him looking for a woman, too. How
could a man look for a woman when he was still searching
for himself?

He stood at the window for hours, watching as night gave
way to dawn. At six, exhausted, he fell on his bed and slept.
When he opened his eyes, it was after nine.

Tyler reached for the telephone.

"Carol," he said, when his secretary answered, "you remember that private detective we used last year? The one who
found out who was selling our research plans to our compet-
itors? I'd like his name, please, and his phone number. No,

no that's fine. I'll call him myself.'' A moment passed. Then
Tyler scrawled down the name and number his secretary gave
him. ''Thank you,'' he said.

He disconnected, took a deep breath and dialed.

CHAPTER TWO

CAITLIN MCCORD had a passion for horses, dogs and kittens
but, because she was a reasonably sane woman, she didn't like
them all in one place at the same time, especially if the dog
was barking, the horse was rolling its eyes and the kitten was
hissing like a rattlesnake.

The horse, a chestnut mare with the unlikely name of
Charlotte, was beautiful, terrified and new to Espada. Caitlin
had spent the best part of half an hour rubbing her velvet nose
and feeding her carrots while she told her they were destined
to be friends. When the mare nuzzled her shoulder, Caitlin
smiled, led her from the stables to the paddock and saddled
her.

That was when the dog, a black-and-tan hound with a clever
nose and a foolish disposition, came wandering by.

"Woof?" said the dog.

The mare rolled her eyes and danced backward. Caitlin held
firmly to the bridle, calmed the horse, shooed the dog and
devoted another five minutes to telling her life was not as
awful as she imagined. When the horse nuzzled her again, she
decided it was time to ease herself gently into the saddle.

That was the moment the dog reappeared, this time in hot
pursuit of a ball of hissing orange fluff.

Caitlin felt the mare's muscles bunch beneath her thighs.
The animal whinnied, reared and pawed the air before she
brought it under control again.

Abel Jones, Espada's foreman, had been watching the go-
ings-on from his window at the eastern end of the stables. He
stepped out the side door into the paddock and spat a thin
stream of tobacco juice into the grass.

"Ornery critter, that horse."

"She just needs to run off some steam."

"Manuel ain't doin' nothin' much this mornin'." Able spat another stream of juice down toward his boots. "He'll take her out, if you like."

Caitlin shot a grin in Abel's direction. "And spoil my fun?" She leaned forward, ran a gloved hand over the chestnut's quivering, arched neck. "I'll do it. Just toss me my hat—it fell off when this little girl tried to make like Trigger."

The old man bent down, plucked the Texas Rangers base- ball cap from the dust, dusted it against his thigh and handed it up. Caitlin pulled the cap on, tucked her dark auburn curls up under it and tugged the brim down over her eyes.

"Open the gate, please."

"Sure you don't want to give Manuel somethin' to do?"

"Open it, Abel."

The foreman grunted. There was no mistaking an order, even when it was issued in a quiet voice.

"Yes, ma'am," he said, and flung the gate to the paddock wide. Horse and woman shot through in a blur.

"That there mare's a wild one," Manuel said, coming up alongside. "Think the *señorita* can handle her?"

Abel's narrowed eyes stayed locked on the receding figures of horse and rider. "She'll handle the mare, all right." He worked the mouthful of chewing tobacco into his cheek, spat and wiped his pepper-and-salt mustache on his sleeve. "It's a stallion's gonna give her trouble, someday."

Manuel gave the foreman a puzzled look. "We got a new stallion? Nobody told me about it."

The old man laughed. "It's what they call a figger of speech, kid."

"A what?"

Abel sighed, reached for a pitchfork and thrust it at the boy.

"Go muck out the stalls," he said, and stomped away.

Tyler Kincaid was driving a battered old Chevy pickup along an unpaved road that undulated through the Texas countryside.

He'd paid some old geezer four hundred bucks for the truck after the plane he'd chartered had flown him to a small airfield just outside town. The P.I. he'd hired said there was a private landing strip on the Baron ranch but Tyler had decided that a man reconnoitering a situation was better off doing it without drawing too much attention to himself. That was why he'd dressed inconspicuously, not in a suit and tie but in weekend clothes—faded jeans and a cotton T-shirt. He'd even resurrected his old Stetson and his roper boots from the back of his closet.

Tyler had figured he could rent a car someplace near the airstrip but he'd figured wrong, which was how he'd ended up with the Chevy. The old truck groaned and rattled like the bucket of bolts it was, and there was dust kicking up through the holes in the floorboard and settling like tan snow on his boots but according to the map in his bag, he didn't have far to go. It was only another ten or twelve miles to the Baron ranch.

The radio worked, anyway. Tyler fiddled with the dial, settled for a station playing the kind of country music he hadn't listened to since his years breaking horses in the hot Georgia sun, first at Boys Ranch and then on his own, after he'd left the Marines. The sentimental songs were made for the hard life of a cowboy. Right now, he just wanted them to take his mind off what he'd set out to do because he suspected that if he thought about it too long, he might admit he was making a mistake.

Why pay a private investigator to dig into the circumstances of his birth and then go out on his own? It was foolish, maybe foolhardy...but this was his life. If anybody was going to find the answers he sought, it was going to be—

The engine hiccuped, made a noise like a sick elephant and came to a convulsive stop.

Tyler frowned, did a quick appraisal of the dashboard gauges. Gas was okay and so was the oil. The engine temperature read normal. He waited a couple of seconds, then turned the key.

"Dammit," he said, and flung the door open.

It was hotter than blazes with the sun beating down. A chorus of insects filled the silence with a melody of their own devising.

Tyler walked to the front of the pickup and lifted the hood, springing back as steam spewed into the already humid air. He mouthed an oath, waited until the cloud dissipated, then leaned forward and peered at the engine. It was a mess. Rust and dirt, frayed wires and worn hoses... It was years since he'd done much more than pump gas into his Porsche but he reached right in. There were some things a man just didn't forget. Things like how you really couldn't expect to get very far with a radiator that leaked like a sieve, and a temperature gauge that had evidently packed it in a long time ago.

Tyler slammed the hood shut, wiped his hands on his jeans and tried not to think about the old codger back at the airstrip, who had to be looking at his four hundred bucks and laughing his head off.

"Hell," he said, and then he sighed. It was his fault, nobody else's. Any man who'd lost touch with reality enough to think he could breeze into a town that was little more than a wide spot on the road, flash some hundred dollar bills and expect not to be taken, was a jerk.

Now what?

He stepped away from the truck, looked back toward where he'd been and then ahead, toward where he was going. The view both ways was the same, nothing but a rolling, dusty road that stretched from horizon to horizon with tall grass waving on either side and trees backing up the grass. He was halfway between nowhere and no place. It was a great title for a country ballad but not a very useful location otherwise.

Tyler stomped back to the truck. He snatched his hat from the front seat and put it on, yanked the map from his bag and checked it. The road went on straight for a couple of miles before taking a sharp right. According to the P.I., he'd see the wrought-iron gates and longhorn logo that marked the entrance to Baron land just before it did.

Going ahead was the only logical choice. If life had taught him anything, it was that taking a step back was never an option.

Tyler folded the map, tucked it into the bag and looped the straps over one shoulder. He tipped the wide brim of the

Stetson down over his eyes and started walking toward Espada.

Three weeks of digging, and all the P. I. had come up with was the name of the ranch where John Smith had been born. Well, it was something. At least he knew now that John Smith had begun life not in Georgia but in Texas.

That was how he thought of the boy he'd been, as if he and Smith were two separate people. The skinny kid with the ropy muscles who'd had to fight for his place in the world was a stranger to the successful man who had everything he could possibly want.

A jackrabbit zipped across the road ahead, moving so quickly it was almost a blur. Maybe the rabbit had places to be, Tyler thought with a tight smile. If the rabbit didn't, he surely did yet here he was, walking a dirt road in Texas when he had a life to live, a corporation to run...and, if he chose, a relationship to mend. Adrianna had phoned and left a message. It hadn't taken much reading between the lines to realize she'd be willing to take him back, on his terms.

The thing of it was, he wasn't sure that was what he wanted.

She was lovely, and charming, and he'd enjoyed the time he'd been with her, but the affair had run its course. He was willing to admit that was his fault but what Adrianna had said about him wasn't true. There was nothing the matter with him. He *did* feel things. If he never spoke of love, it was simply because he couldn't bring himself to lie.

He liked women, liked their soft laughter and their scent, but that didn't mean he was going to pretend there was more to the best of male-female relationships than a few months of companionship, good times and sex.

Sex was something he never lied about. It was a need, a powerful one, and if you shared it with a beautiful, interesting, willing woman, it was one of the most pleasurable things in life.

A smile curled across the corner of Tyler's mouth. Finding women to adorn his arm and warm his bed had never been a problem.

For now, though, he was going to concentrate his energies

on an enigma named John Smith. And Smith *was* an enigma, one not even the detective he'd hired had been able to unravel.

"I have to tell you, Mr. Kincaid," Ed Crane had said, when they'd met for breakfast the prior week, "this is one of the toughest investigations I've ever done."

Tyler's eyed had narrowed. "Meaning?"

"Meaning," Crane had replied, around a mouthful of buttermilk gravy, "all I know is what's in that report I sent you this morning."

"Humor me," Tyler said, with a smile that made the phrase a lie. "I haven't had time to do much besides glance at it. Smith was born in Texas?"

"Uh-huh."

"On a windblown acre of dusty soil?"

"No, sir, Mr. Kincaid. We're talking about a ranch the size of a small country." Crane offered his best good old boy smile. "Anywhere but Texas, this Espada would be flying its own flag. Cattle, horses, oil wells—this isn't any windblown acre. It's a miniature kingdom."

"A kingdom," Tyler said slowly.

"Yes, indeedy. Ruled by an old hard-ass name of Jonas Baron. The guy was eighty-five last summer, he's on wife number five, he's got three sons and a stepdaughter—a kingdom and a king, sir, that's the setup at Espada."

"And John Smith was born there." Tyler eyed Crane over the rim of his coffee cup. "To whom?"

Crane's smile faded. "Well, that's the problem. We haven't been able to turn up a record so far. But there are some strong possibilities."

Tyler put down his coffee cup. "Such as?"

"I'd rather wait until I have all the facts, sir."

"And I wouldn't."

Crane cleared his throat. "Well, there's a housekeeper, woman named Carmen. She was pregnant that winter, would have delivered just about the middle of the summer."

Tyler nodded, waited to feel some reaction but didn't. Whoever his mother had been, she'd dumped him fast enough. Only a fool would feel anything for a woman like that.

"Possibilities, you said."

"Yes, sir. There were a couple of married ranch hands working at the place that summer, one, maybe two, with wives who were expecting."

Tyler smiled stiffly. "A fertile place, this Espada."

Crane grinned. "Yeah."

"Anyone else?"

"Jonas Baron's wife—wife number one—was expecting, too. But that one's easy to rule out."

"Yes. You already said, Baron has three sons."

"He does, Mr. Kincaid, and they were all born after the year you specified." Crane reached for another biscuit, thought better of it and let his jowly face settle into more serious lines. "Besides, the baby and Mrs. Baron both died in childbirth. The two of them are buried out there, on the ranch."

"Which leaves us with the housekeeper and the cowboys."

"That's right, sir. So, what do you think? You want me to keep on digging?"

For a moment, Tyler had been tempted to tell the man to end the investigation. His mother was either a housekeeper or the wife of an itinerant cowboy. Either way, she'd abandoned him with less thought than most people gave to an old shoe. Not that it mattered. He'd done just fine on his own. He wasn't even sure exactly why he'd started this search. He'd been in a strange mood the night of his birthday, that was all.

On the other hand, he'd never been able to resist a puzzle. It was part of the reason he'd succeeded in business. What made people take one path, instead of another? His mother had given birth to him, then dumped him on a doorstep. Why? Why hadn't she turned him over to an adoption agency? And why would a woman rise from the bed where she'd just delivered a child and go all the way to Atlanta to get rid of it?

"Mr. Kincaid? Shall I keep going? Another couple weeks, I'll have a better fix on things. You just need to be patient."

Patient, Tyler had thought. It was a logical suggestion, easy for a man to make when it wasn't his past that was being uncovered but after thirty-five years, what was the rush? But there *was* a rush; he didn't understand it but he could feel it, in his belly. So he'd nodded, told Crane to keep on digging. The meeting had ended, Tyler had returned to his office and buried himself in work.

An hour later, he'd given up pretending. How could a man work when his head was filled with pictures of a place he'd never seen and images of three faceless women, one of whom was probably his mother? He'd called in his personal assistant and his first vice president, told them he was going away for a while and that he'd keep in touch by e-mail and phone. They'd both looked surprised but he knew they wouldn't question him. Nobody ever questioned Tyler Kincaid.

"Fine," his P.A. said.

His vice president shook his hand and wished him a pleasant vacation.

Tyler hadn't bothered correcting him. There wasn't much he could have said that wouldn't have made him look even more surprised, so he'd smiled and said he'd certainly try. And here he was, trudging into a gully on a dusty road in the middle of nowhere, his shirt stuck to his skin with sweat, looking for answers that probably wouldn't matter a damn once he found them.

"Hell," he said, and came to an abrupt stop at the bottom of the slope. Was he crazy? Who gave a damn about John Smith? He'd ceased to exist years ago. What did it matter if—

"Look out!"

He heard the hoofbeats and the cry almost simultaneously, spun around and saw a horse crest the top of the slope and fly toward him. Tyler flung himself out of the way and the animal thundered by with only inches to spare.

Tyler went down in the brush at the side of the road, then he scrambled to his feet. The horse and its rider, a boy who didn't look as if he had enough muscle to control a pony much less a horse that looked as high-strung as this one, were drawing up a couple of dozen yards down the road. The horse turned, blowing hard. The rider rose in the saddle and looked at him.

Tyler waited for some word. An apology. A question. Are you okay? seemed like a good start but the boy didn't speak. He sat down again, straight as a ramrod in the saddle, while the horse blew and snorted. The kid was wearing a baseball cap pulled low over his forehead so he couldn't see his face, but every inch of the boy's posture indicated contempt.

Tyler drew in a breath, enough to calm his runaway heart rate. Then he plucked his hat from the dirt, knocked off the dust and jammed it on his head as he moved into the center of the road..

"You damned near ran me down," he yelled.

The horse tossed its head. The boy said nothing. Tyler tucked his hands into his back pockets and walked toward them.

"Hey, kid, did you hear me? I said—"

"I heard what you said." The boy's voice was low. There was an edge to it that suggested he was accustomed to giving orders. "You're trespassing."

"This is a public road."

"It's a private road. Or am I supposed to believe you opened the gate three miles back, walked under the arch and never noticed?"

Tyler frowned. He hadn't come through any gate that he knew of though he supposed it was possible, considering how lost in thought he'd been.

"Well? Is that your story, cowboy?"

Tyler's frown deepened. The kid's voice had an interesting quality to it, one that sent a funny sensation dancing along his spine. A couple of dark auburn curls had escaped from the baseball cap he was wearing. No, not dark auburn. Red, and chestnut; maple and even a touch of gold…

Holy hell. He must have been out in the sun longer than he thought. It would be a hot day at the North Pole before he cared one way or another about the sound of a boy's voice, or the color of his hair.

The horse whinnied and danced sideways. "Did I say something that amuses you?" the boy asked coldly.

"I didn't see any gate," Tyler said, just as coldly. "Not

that it matters a damn. Public land or private, you haven't the right to—''

The boy touched his knees lightly to the chestnut's sides. The horse took half a dozen steps forward. Tyler had been away from horses for a long time but the animal had a look that said it had a touchy disposition and, probably, a hair-trigger temper.

"If the gate was open, it's because some no-account left it that way and I assure you, I'll deal with him.''

"Yeah," Tyler said slowly, his eyes locked to the rider's shadowed face, "I'll just bet you will."

"You just turn around now and head back out the way you came.''

The presumptive quality of that throaty voice, the command issued by a skinny boy who couldn't have been a day older than, what, sixteen, seventeen, made Tyler's muscles knot.

"You're pretty good at giving orders," he said softly. "What happens when you run into a man who won't take them?''

The boy hesitated, then touched his knees to the chestnut's sides again. The horse moved closer, as much a weapon now as if the boy had picked up a stone.

"You mean, what happens when I run into a fool that doesn't use the brain he was born with?''

"Yeah," Tyler said, and in one quick move he reached up and grabbed the boy by the front of his T-shirt. The chestnut whinnied and danced away but Tyler hung on and hauled the kid from the saddle…

Except, as soon as he'd dragged him halfway down the length of his body, he knew it wasn't a boy at all.

It was a woman.

A slender woman, but one who had all the right parts in all the right places. Round, high breasts that pressed against his chest. Rounded hips that meshed with his. An incredible mass of silky auburn hair that fell to her shoulders when her baseball cap dropped to the grass. Enormous hazel eyes, the irises shot with green and gold, stared into his; delicate bones and surprisingly hard muscle twisted under his hands.

"Damn you," she gasped, "let go of me!"

Her skin was hot, and so was the smell of her. Sweat, horse, summer meadows and woman...she smelled of things he'd once known and things he'd never had, and the feel of her against him, of those soft breasts and narrow hips, of that tilted pelvis and the long, endless legs, turned him as hard as stone.

She felt his erection. She had to. He had her trapped against him. He saw her eyes darken, saw her mouth tremble. What the hell are you doing, Kincaid? he asked himself coldly, but even as he asked it, he wondered what would happen if he tumbled her down into the soft grass, how long it would take to strip the clothes from her, touch her, turn the anger and growing fear in her eyes to need...

Tyler dropped his hands from her and took a step back.

"A woman's an idiot," he said roughly, "to take on something that's too much for her to handle."

Caitlin's heart was slamming against her ribs. Was he talking about the horse or about what had just happened between them? All her talk about this being private land was just that. Talk. What did a man like this care if he were trespassing? She was alone out here. And even though she was strong and fit, she'd be defenseless against a man like this. She'd felt all that tightly leashed power, that almost-terrifying maleness... and she'd felt something else, too, something even more frightening. For a heartbeat, as he held her, she'd felt like a sleeping cat coming slowly awake under the expert stroke of a man's hand.

Heat rushed under her skin. She covered it by bending down and retrieving her cap. When she looked up again, her face gave nothing away. The only way to handle the situation was to show no fear, even though her heart was still banging like a drum.

"I assure you," she said crisply, "I can handle the chestnut. As for you—if you turn around right now and walk on out, I won't report you."

"Report me?" He laughed. "Damn, but you're good at this, lady. We're in the ass-end of nowhere, and you're making threats."

"We're on private land, as I've already told you. And I make promises, not threats." Caitlin looked him over, from head to toe. He was a drifter. The battered old hat, the worn boots, the very fact that he was traveling on foot through the hot Texas countryside...but there was something about him. It wasn't just his looks: The long, muscular legs. The narrow hips and broad shoulders. The face that was handsome in a dark, dangerous way. It was more than that. The way he held himself, maybe, or the way he looked at her out of those emerald-green eyes. There was an authority to him—and that was ridiculous. Drifters had no authority, no aura of command...

"Do I pass muster?"

Her gaze flew to his. He was watching her from under his sooty lashes, arms folded, his expression unreadable. She could feel herself blushing again but she fought against it and against the desire to turn away from that penetrating stare.

"Texas is filled with men like you," she said.

"Really." He shifted his weight, tucked his hands into his back pockets. "And what kind of man is that?"

"You're broke, you need a job, a place to sleep and eat."

Tyler started to laugh but thought better of it. Behind her, the chestnut eyed them warily, its reins trailing through a bed of wildflowers.

"And?"

"And, we don't hire drifters. You're not going to find work at Espada."

He jerked as if she'd slapped him. Espada. Of course. He'd been so damned caught up in playing games with the woman...

"Espada," he said softly. His eyes met hers. "You're Caitlin McCord. Baron's stepdaughter."

This time, she was the one who looked surprised. "How do you know that?"

"Everybody knows it," Tyler said, cursing himself for the slip. He shrugged lazily. "People talk. After all, Espada's the biggest spread in the county."

"Then you must also know that what I told you is true. We don't hire—"

"Baron's the man I've come to see."

"You can't. He's not here."

"I'll wait."

"He won't be back for days."

"And I just said, I'll wait."

"It's a free country. You want to wait, wait, but not on Baron land."

She swung away from him. It was a gesture of complete dismissal. Tyler stared at that straight back, the stiff shoulders, and his composure snapped. He reached out, grabbed her arm and swung her toward him.

"Dammit," he growled, "don't you turn your back on—"

The sudden movement, or maybe the anger in his voice, were too much for the nervous horse. The chestnut jerked back, tossed her head and reared. Caitlin didn't see it happen but she might as well have. She felt the whisper of air as the animal moved, saw the flash of awareness in the drifter's eyes, and then he yelled a warning, caught her by the shoulders and tumbled her to the ground, rolling her out from under those slashing hooves.

They lay in the grass, tangled together, his hard, long body pinning hers beneath it.

"You okay?" he said, and when she nodded, then managed a shaky "yes," he scrambled to his feet and made a grab for the mare's reins.

Caitlin stood up, dusted off her bottom and watched. The chestnut whinnied, fought, but the stranger hung on, the muscles in his arms and shoulders bunching under his T-shirt. The horse was strong but the man was stronger. After a few minutes, the animal trembled and calmed. The stranger rubbed the mare's throat. He stroked the trembling neck and spoke softly.

The chestnut's body shuddered, then became still. She pressed her head to the man's shoulder.

"She's okay now," he said quietly.

Caitlin cleared her throat. "Yes. I... I... Thank you. She's new, you see, and scared..."

"She's new and scared, and needs to know who's boss."
The chestnut blew softly. "Isn't that right, girl?"

"You—you seem to know horses."

The stranger's smile didn't reach his eyes. "What else
would a man like me know, Ms. McCord?"

Women, Caitlin thought. That was what a man like him
would know. A tremor raced through her, and she looked
away.

"So, what do you think? Can you use an extra hand who
knows his way around horses?"

Caitlin ran the tip of her tongue over her lips. "Look, I'm—
I'm grateful for what you just did, mister, but—"

"Kincaid. My name's Tyler Kincaid."

He held out his hand. She looked at it, looked at him, told
herself it was ridiculous to feel heat sweep over her skin again.

"Ms. McCord?"

Slowly she put her hand in his. His fingers clasped hers
tightly. They were warm and strong, but she already knew how
gentle they could be. She'd seen the way he stroked the mare.
Would he touch a woman's skin the same way?

Color flew into her cheeks and she jerked back her hand.
"All right," she said briskly. "I'll give you a week's trial.
The ranch is a couple of miles beyond that ridge. Talk to Abel.
He's our foreman. Tell him... Hey. Hey, Kincaid! What are
you doing?"

The question was pointless because he'd already done it.
Tyler Kincaid had swung into the saddle. Now, he was holding
his hand out to her, as if the horse and the land were his and
she were the trespasser.

"You wouldn't ask a man to walk in this heat, would you?"

He gave her a slow smile, the sort that made it clear she'd
seem incredibly foolish to say yes, she would, if he were the
man in question.

With a hiss of breath, Caitlin put her hand in Tyler's and
swung up into the saddle behind him. He'd saved her from
injury or worse but she'd made a mistake, she knew that now,
even if it was too late to do anything about it.

"Hang on," he said, which she had no intention of doing.

But he leaned low over the horse's neck, whispered something and the animal took off like the wind. Caitlin had no choice but to wrap her arms tightly around Tyler's waist as they raced toward Espada.

CHAPTER THREE

THE woman had been easy to convince—but then, it was she who'd come up with the story, not he.

By the third morning of his employment at Espada, Tyler was almost ready to believe the tale himself. Once, a long time ago, a lifetime ago, he'd been an itinerant cowboy, wandering from ranch to ranch, taking a job here, another there, doing whatever needed doing so he could put a meal in his belly.

That was the man he'd been, the man Caitlin McCord thought he was. And he, lacking any better entrée to the Baron kingdom, and to whatever secrets it might hold, had accepted the scenario.

The only person who didn't buy into it was the foreman.

Tyler knew those keen old eyes had not missed the way he and Caitlin McCord had come riding in together on the horse, and certainly not the way she'd jumped from the saddle, her face pale, her eyes cold.

"This is Tyler Kincaid," she'd said to the old man, as Tyler strolled after her. "Give him a job, a bed and a meal."

She turned on her heel and stalked off toward the main house, shoulders set, spine rigid. Tyler watched her go and thought how remarkable it was that a woman could look so stiffly unyielding when she felt so softly feminine in a man's arms.

"Kincaid."

The old man's voice had sounded rough as gravel. Tyler looked at him.

"Ms. Caitlin ain't an employee. She's family."

The warning was clear.

"And she's offered me a job," Tyler said, smiling politely.

"So she has." The old man's face was expressionless.

35

"Name's Jones," he said, and spat into the dirt. "Abel Jones. I'm the foreman here."

Tyler nodded, started to stick out his hand and thought better of it.

"Where'd you work last?"

"Here and there," Tyler answered, with a lazy smile.

"You ain't from these parts."

"No," Tyler agreed, "I'm not."

"Southerner, ain't you?"

"Yeah. From Georgia. But I was born in Texas."

It was the first time Tyler had said such a thing, or even thought it. The old man stared at him for a long moment, his eyes narrowed to slits.

"Fancy duffel you got there," he said, jerking his whiskered chin at Tyler's bag.

Tyler didn't blink. "Nylon. Lasts longer than canvas."

"Uh-huh. What can you do?"

"Rope, ride, fix whatever needs fixing. And I'm good with horses." God, he'd said those same words more times than he wanted to remember, a thousand years ago.

"Ms. Caitlin wants you hired on, so be it." The foreman's eyes turned flinty. "Jes do your job and we'll get along fine."

Tyler recognized the warning that was implicit in the simple words. But he said nothing, simply nodded and followed a kid named Manuel to the bunkhouse, where he was assigned a room.

"You want me to show you around?" the kid asked.

"No, that's okay. I want to put my stuff away first."

Abel was waiting for him, shovel in hand when he came out, but Tyler ignored it.

"I'm hungry," he said shortly. "Haven't eaten in a long time."

Well, it wasn't a lie. He'd had breakfast hours ago. Half a grapefruit, a croissant, black coffee. His usual morning meal, sufficient when a man faced a few hours spent riding a desk and then lunch with a client but not very substantive when you were going to ride horses or clean up after them, he thought grimly, looking at the foreman and the shovel.

The old man nodded. "You don't look much like you've missed a meal."

Tyler forced a smile. "Care to listen to my stomach growl, Pop?"

"Name's Abel. All right, go on up to the main house, to the back door. Tell Carmen to feed you."

The house on the rise was big and imposing, but no more so than Tyler's own home back in Atlanta. He concentrated on the irony in that in hopes it would keep him from thinking about the banging of his own heart as he rapped on the door, then stepped inside to confront the woman who might have borne him.

Carmen was round. Round face, round body—even her shiny black hair was round, braided and twisted high on her head in a coronet.

And she was not his mother. Tyler knew it, the minute she turned from the stove and smiled at him.

"Señor?"

"Abel sent me," he told her, while his heartbeat returned to normal. "He said it would be okay if you fixed me something to eat."

She smiled even more broadly, sat him at a massive oak table and fed him *huevos rancheros,* homemade biscuits and cups of fragrant black coffee until he thought he'd burst.

"The men who work at Espada are lucky to have you to cook for them. Your children, too," he said casually, because he needed to be certain, even though he already knew.

"Ah, my children," Carmen said happily, and told him all about Esme, her daughter, who was twenty and in her second year at the university, and about her son, Esteban, who was a doctor in Austin.

"Dr. Esteban O'Connor," she said, and chuckled. A blush colored her dusky cheeks, making her look younger than her years. "The child of my youth—and of a youthful indiscretion."

Tyler smiled. "And how old is this child of your youth?" he said, even more casually, and Carmen told him that Esteban was going to celebrate his thirty-fifth birthday next month.

Tyler had nodded, tried to ignore the sudden emptiness inside. It wasn't a surprise; he'd known, hadn't he, that this warmhearted woman wasn't his mother? She'd never have given him life, then abandoned him.

"That was a wonderful meal," he'd said. "*Gracias,* Carmen."

He'd dropped a kiss on her cheek and gone to find Abel, who'd set him to work.

Work was what the old man had given him, all right, Tyler thought now, grunting as he unloaded feed sacks from the back of a pickup truck. Hard work, too, as if hoisting heavy sacks and shoveling manure were tests he had to pass before he could be trusted with anything as important as risking his neck trying to break a horse.

All the time he worked, whatever the job, he kept his eyes open, alert for something, anything, that might give him some clue about his birth, about how his mother—his parents—had fit into the enormous puzzle that was Espada. He knew it was foolish, that he'd left this place when he was only a day or two old. What memories would a newborn infant have? Not a one. He understood that.

Still, he looked at everything as if the most simple thing could be the key to unlock the mystery of his past.

And then, on the third morning, Caitlin McCord came strolling toward the stable and he knew he'd been kidding himself. Part of him had been searching for clues to John Smith's birth—but part of him had been watching, and waiting, for her.

He felt as if someone had landed a hard right to his jaw.

She was beautiful. How in the world had he ever mistaken her for a boy, even at a distance?

It was a hot day. China-blue sky, brutal yellow sun, with no breeze or a cloud to ease the sizzling temperature. He was sweating and so were the other men. Even the horses were feeling the heat, but Caitlin looked untouched by it.

He drank in the sight of her. She was wearing a sleeveless blue T-shirt and he could see the musculature of her arms, the strength of them, and he wondered why it was that he'd never before thought how sexy that could be. She was wearing jeans, as he was, but hers were a faded blue, almost white at the knees and hems. They fit her snugly, cupping her bottom, skimming the length of those incredibly long, long legs as lovingly as a caress. Her hair was pulled back from her face but a couple of auburn curls had escaped at her ears and on her forehead.

Tyler drew in his breath.

She looked, he thought, like a cool, clear drink of water—and he was a man dying of thirst.

He tossed the last sack from the truck, then straightened up. She was going to pass within a couple of feet of him and the truck but her gaze never drifted right or left. His belly clenched. She was going to walk right on by and pretend he wasn't even there.

To hell with that, he thought, and jumped down in front of her.

"Good morning."

Caitlin stumbled to a halt. "Good morning," she said coolly, and started around him. Tyler moved along with her.

"Nice day," he said.

"Very." She took a step to the right. Tyler took a step, too.

"Mr. Kincaid—"

"Well," he said lazily, "isn't that something? When I was trespassin' on your property, you called me 'Kincaid,' but now that I'm gainfully in your employ, I've graduated to 'Mr.'"

Caitlin flashed him a look. "It isn't my property, Mr. Kincaid, nor are you in my employ. This ranch belongs to Jonas Baron."

"You're his stepdaughter."

"Exactly."

"Beggin' your pardon, but I don't see the difference."

"I am not a Baron, Mr. Kincaid. That means I hold no legal interest in Espada and never will. Now, if you'll excuse me—"

"Is there a reason you've been avoidin' me, Ms. McCord?"

Caitlin flushed. "I haven't been... I don't like being made fun of, Mr. Kincaid."

"Forgive me, Ms. McCord. I wasn't makin' fun, I was makin' an observation."

"Here's an observation for you, Kincaid." Her hazel eyes flashed as she looked at him. "I find it interesting that you seem to have developed a drawl in the last couple of days. And you can ditch the 'forgive me's' and the 'beggin' your pardon' nonsense. Expressions like those are lies, coming from you. I don't think you've ever apologized to anybody in your life."

Tyler tried to look wounded. "I'm a Southerner, Ms. McCord. We're all gentlemen. Would a gentleman lie to a lady?"

He saw her mouth twitch but she stopped the smile before it got started. "You didn't talk that way when we met, Kincaid."

He grinned. "Maybe I was trying to impress you."

"Maybe you were trying to convince me you were something you're not."

Tyler's dark brows lifted. "Meaning?"

"Meaning, Abel doesn't think you're who you claim to be, and I'm starting to think he's right."

"Because of the way I talk?"

"Because of the way you act, Kincaid. Everything about you says you're not the drifter you pretend to be." Her nostrils flared. "And because you're the first hand we've ever hired who has a cell phone in his duffel bag."

Tyler bit back the curse that rose to his lips. "And you're the first employer who's gone through my things."

"One of the men saw you using it." She put her hands on her hips and looked into his eyes. "Or are you going to deny the phone is yours?"

"No point denying it."

He reached past her for his shirt, which he'd left hanging on the tailgate. The scent of him rose to her nostrils, a combination of sun and man, and his arm brushed lightly against hers. Caitlin felt her heartbeat stumble, which was ridiculous. She didn't trust Tyler Kincaid, didn't like him—and she surely didn't enjoy standing this close to him when he was half-naked. Lots of the men worked shirtless on a day like this but that didn't mean he couldn't have had the decency to cover up before he spoke to her instead of putting his body on display.

At least now he'd put his shirt on, rolled up the sleeves, smoothed down the collar. Dammit, why didn't he do up the buttons? She certainly had no wish to look at the dark hair on his chest, or follow it as it arrowed down toward his belly button, over those hard abdominal muscles...

"Ms. McCord?"

There was a little tilt to the corner of his mouth and she knew, she *knew,* he'd done it deliberately, put himself on exhibit as if she gave a damn what his body looked like, or how many women had known the pleasure of it.

"Lots of things are against the law," he said softly. "This isn't one of them."

She flushed. "I beg your pardon?"

"I said, owning a portable phone isn't illegal."

Caitlin straightened her spine. "You're not a drifter," she said flatly.

Tyler answered with a shrug.

"Why did you say you were?"

"You were the one who called me that, lady. Not me."

"You didn't try to correct me, Kincaid."

"Correct you?" He laughed. "'You want to wait,'" he said, mimicking her, "'wait, but not on Baron land.' You were into your Lady of the Manor routine. I figured correcting you would only have landed my butt in jail for trespass."

Her color heightened but she kept her chin up and her indignation intact. "Who are you, then? And what do you want at Espada?"

He hesitated. He could tell her the truth, tell her the reason he'd come here, but the survival instincts he'd honed years before, that had kept him in one piece at the State Home and then in covert operations in the steaming jungles of Central America, were too powerful to let him make such a mistake. There were secrets here; he was certain of it. There was something in the way Abel looked at him, in the way Caitlin spoke of her role at Espada...

"Kincaid? I asked you a question. What do you want?"

He looked at the woman standing before him. Her eyes were almost gold in the morning sun; her hair was a hundred different shades of red and mahogany and maple. Her mouth was free of lipstick, full and innocent-looking, and he wondered what she'd say, what she'd do, if he told her that what he wanted, ever since he'd laid eyes on her, was to take her in his arms, tumble her into the grass, strip off that cold and haughty look, and the boyish clothes with which she camouflaged a woman's body, and ignite the heat he knew smoldered in her blood.

Hell, he thought, and turned away.

"I told you what I wanted," he said roughly. Grunting, he hoisted a feed sack on his shoulder and walked into the stable. "I want to talk to Jonas Baron."

"About what?"

Tyler dumped the sack and headed out the door. "It's none of your business."

"Everything about this ranch is my business."

"You just told me otherwise. You're not a Baron, you said, remember?"

"I run Espada, Kincaid. Maybe you'd better get that through your head."

It took all his determination not to turn around and show her that she might damned well run this ranch but she didn't run him. This was a woman who needed to be reminded that she was a woman, and he ached for the chance to give her that reminder, but he knew it would be a mistake. Instead he decided to take the wind out of her sails.

"That's fine," he said easily, "but my business with Baron has nothing to do with Espada. Now, if you're done questioning me, Ms. McCord, I've got these sacks to deal with and the stalls to muck out, so if it's all the same with you—"

"Stalls? What about the horses?"

"What about them?"

"Why aren't you working with the stock?"

"Ask Abel. I'm sure he's a font of information." He brushed past her on his way out the door.

"I told him you're good with horses," she said as she followed him back and forth. "And he knows we have a horse that needs gentling—*oof*."

"Sorry." Tyler caught her by the elbows as she tottered backward.

"That's—that's all right..."

Her heart rose into her throat. His hands were still on her. His eyes glinted like jewels in the shadowed darkness of the stable. And, as she looked into their green depths, she saw something that sent her pulse racing.

"I'll speak with him," she said. "With Abel. About putting you to better use."

A smile curved his mouth, one so sexy and dangerous that it made her breath stop.

"Good." His voice was soft and slightly husky. A shudder ripped along her spine as he looked down at her mouth, then into her eyes. "I'd like to be put to better use."

"With—with the horses."

The smile came again, lazy and even more dangerous. "Of course."

Caitlin knew she was blushing and hated herself for it, hated this insufferably egotistical male even more for causing her face to redden.

"Let go of me, please."

"Ever the lady," he said, in that same husky whisper. "Except, I don't believe it. I think there are times you're not quite the lady you pretend to be."

"I am always a lady," she said coldly.

"In that case..." His hands slid up her arms and clasped her shoulders. "Maybe it's time somebody showed you what you're missing, Ms. McCord."

"Kincaid." Was that breathless little voice really hers? Caitlin cleared her throat. "Kincaid, take your hands off me."

"I would," he said lazily. "But that's not what you really want, is it?"

"Listen, you—you arrogant, egotistical—"

"Kincaid? Kincaid, where in hell are you?"

Abel's voice, and the echo of his footsteps on the cement floor, cut through the building tension. Tyler let his hands fall from Caitlin's shoulders. He stepped aside and she slipped past him, just as the foreman stepped into the stable.

The old man looked from her to Tyler. "Is there a problem, Ms. Caitlin?"

"Yes." Caitlin shot Tyler an angry look. "Yes, there is. I want you to tell this man…to tell him…" She looked at Tyler, whose gaze had not left her, and her throat tightened. "Starting tomorrow, let him work with the horses. With the new mare that's afraid of her own shadow. You hear me, Abel?"

Abel's bushy brows shot up, but he nodded. "Yes, ma'am. I'll see to it."

Caitlin stood leaning against the railing of the small corral, watching Tyler and the horse and wishing she'd followed her instincts and fired him. But she'd called Jonas in New York, and Jonas had told her to let him stay on.

"Man's up to somethin', Catie," Jonas had said. "You keep him there till I get back. Just you watch yourself, you hear? Don't turn your back."

She'd been careful not to do that. In fact, she'd made it a point to keep an eye on Kincaid. Just now, others were doing the same thing, including Abel, leaning on the rail beside her.

"Man's got good hands," he said, and spat into the dust.

"Yes," she said, with an indifferent shrug. She didn't want to think about those hands, about how they'd felt on her. "He seems to." She cleared her throat. "I was wondering if you had any ideas about putting Lancelot to stud."

"Did you ask him what he's doin' here? Man like that ain't no drifter."

"He's here to talk with Jonas."

"And to shovel manure?" Abel snorted. "I don't think so."

"Look, Abel, Tyler Kincaid isn't our problem. He wanted a job, we gave him a job, and he's doing it, isn't he?"

"Suppose he is. But he asks a lot of questions."

"Questions?" Caitlin looked at the foreman. "About what?"

Abel lifted his shoulders. "This, that. Everythin'. Asked Carmen to tell him about herself, her kids. Asked a couple of the older men if they'd been workin' here long, what they knew of the old days, how it was on Espada then."

Caitlin smiled despite herself. "Dangerous questions, huh? I mean, a man's definitely up to no good if he wants to talk about the old days, or if he takes the time to ask Carmen about her son and daughter."

"Just figured I'd let you know what's going' on, Ms. Caitlin. Everythin' ain't always what it seems."

"I appreciate that," she said gently. She looked at Tyler, watched the mare come forward daintily to sniff at the hand he held out to her. "He's probably just a cowboy that's got some get-rich-quick scheme he's dying to tell Jonas about." She smiled. "And we both know how Jonas will deal with that."

The foreman chuckled. "Yes, ma'am. Tyler Kincaid'll be out of here so fast it'll make his head spin."

Caitlin turned back to the corral as Abel sauntered away. She stepped up on the bottom rail and watched Tyler's performance.

That was what it was, all right. A performance, but she had to admit, it was enjoyable. Tyler had a gentle touch, strong hands and a sense of authority. The mare was responding to all of it.

Just as she had.

The thought made her uneasy, and she forced it from her head.

The sun had climbed higher; it was a blazing fist of yellow, punching through the blue sky. Tyler had left his shirt on and it was soaked through. Caitlin could see the muscles move and bunch beneath the wet fabric. Her face heated; she looked sideways at the men lining the fence but all their attention was on the man and the horse. Some of the men called out good-natured words of advice.

Tyler looked at them, smiled, even grinned—but he never once looked at her.

It annoyed her, though she knew it was silly. Why should he look at her? Still, it ticked her off. A while ago, she'd accused him of being arrogant because of the way he'd spoken to her. Now, she was thinking of him as arrogant because he refused to acknowledge her presence. She was being an idiot...except, dammit, he *was* being arrogant. She knew it. Did he think it was a turn-on? Caitlin thumbed her hair behind her ears. Not for her, it wasn't. She'd grown up watching her mother succumb to a seemingly endless succession of men whose egos were bigger than their IQs. Even Jonas, who was as smart as a whip, thought he could strut through life with only his arrogance to guide him.

If Tyler Kincaid thought the same thing, he was in for a nasty surprise.

Eventually the mare was trembling with exhaustion. Tyler rubbed her ears, whispered to her, then jerked his head toward Manuel, who was watching with the others.

"She's had enough for today," he told the boy. "Take her inside. Give her a good rubdown and some of those special oats she's so fond of."

Caitlin waited for Manuel to point out that Tyler could take the mare inside himself, that he was nobody to give orders, but the boy nodded and did as he'd been told. The same thing had happened when Tyler began working with the mare. One of the older men had been standing around, smoking. Tyler had asked him to get the mare's tack and Pete hadn't hesitated, even though he was as independent in spirit as most cowboys.

There was an art to giving men like this orders, and some basic rules.

Rule number one was that one ranch hand didn't give an order to another but the men seemed to have forgotten that. Tyler asked a man to do something, the man did it. It was as simple as that.

And it annoyed the hell out of her. Was she supposed to stand by and let a stranger order her men around? Jonas had

told her to keep Kincaid on until he got back but that didn't
mean she had to let him march all over her.

It was time to push things and find out who Kincaid really
was, and what he wanted.

The men drifted away. Kincaid strolled toward her. He had
the lazy walk of a man who spent lots of time in the saddle
but it was tempered with a masculine grace and innate authority she'd never seen in anyone but Jonas Baron and her
stepbrothers. Strange, that she should think of Jonas's sons
just now, and yet—and yet, there was something so familiar
in that walk. In the set of those shoulders...

"Show's over," Tyler said. "You can leave now."

Color flooded her face. She took her arms from the top rail
and stepped back. "What did you say?"

That smile she'd seen before—insolent, all-knowing, dangerously sexy—curved across his mouth. He opened the gate
and stepped out of the corral.

"You heard me. I said the show was over."

Caitlin could feel herself tremble with anger. She watched
as he drew his shirt over his head and used it to mop his torso.
Sun glinted on his chest, touched the powerful muscles of his
biceps, the ridged abdominal wall with gold.

Her mouth thinned. "Must you flaunt yourself?"

"It's hot. I've been working my tail off. If that means I'm
flaunting myself, so be it."

"You're out of line, Kincaid."

"I'm honest, Ms. McCord."

"You're insolent, and you're so full of yourself it's a miracle you don't explode."

"So I've been told."

"I'll just bet you have." Caitlin blew a strand of hair from
her forehead and bunched her fists on her hips. "Just what are
you doing here, Kincaid?"

"Hell, Ms. McCord, we've been over this ground already."

"Yes, and you told me it was none of my affair but I think
it is. I want some answers, and I want them now."

"I told you, I have business with Jonas Baron." Tyler hung

the shirt over his shoulder, hooked it on his thumb and started toward the bunkhouse. Caitlin fell in beside him.

"What kind of business?" Her legs were long, but his were longer. She was almost running to keep up with him, and she didn't like it. "Dammit," she said, dancing out in front of him, "stand still when I'm talking to you!"

Tyler's eyes narrowed. "Do you use that tone of voice with all your hands?"

"Just answer the question, Kincaid. What are you doing at Espada?"

Tyler looked down into Caitlin's face. It was flushed and her hazel eyes glittered with anger—and he was pretty sure he knew what that anger was all about. She'd been watching him work the mare. Hell, she'd been watching him ever since yesterday. After three days of never so much as glimpsing her, he saw her everywhere. And each time he did, he could feel her eyes on him. Not that he could ever catch her looking. The second he turned toward her, Caitlin McCord swung away like a nervous filly.

A muscle danced in his jaw.

And he knew the reason.

Something had ignited between them, hot and electric, primitive, almost pagan. What he wanted, what she wanted, was to feel him deep inside her. He knew it. She knew it—and she didn't like it.

She was too good for him. She thought so, anyway. He'd been watching her as she went about her business and yeah, she knew her way around the ranch. She wasn't afraid of getting her hands dirty or her boots soiled, and there was muscle tucked away beneath that soft, golden skin, but that didn't mean she wasn't a lady.

And ladies didn't stoop to play bedroom games with the likes of the man she thought he was, the man he would have been, if he were still John Smith.

"Dammit, Kincaid, I asked you a question!"

Tyler turned away abruptly, walked to the old-fashioned horse trough beside the bunkhouse and ducked his head into the cool water.

"And I answered it," he said, looking at her.

He ran his fingers through his hair, spearing it back from his face, and blotted his face with his shirt. She tried not to notice the drops of water, caught like diamonds, that glittered against his tanned shoulders and clung to the dark mat of hair on his chest.

"You don't belong here."

His teeth showed in a quick smile. "No?"

"No. You're no cowhand."

He sighed, leaned back against the trough and folded his arms. "Look, lady, I didn't storm the castle walls. You said Baron wasn't here, you offered me a job and I took it. Why make it into anything more complicated than that?"

"Maybe," Caitlin said stiffly, "I made a mistake."

His eyes turned dark. "Maybe you did." He took a step forward. "Truth is," he said softly, "this hasn't anything to do with you wanting to know why I came to Espada, does it?"

"Certainly it does. I'm in charge, when Jonas is away, and—"

"It's me." His voice was low. He moved forward again and she took a step back. "I make you uneasy."

"Don't be silly. I'm not afraid of you."

Tyler smiled. "No?"

"No. Of course I'm not. I—"

"Maybe you're afraid of yourself."

She caught her breath as he reached out and lay his hand against her cheek. It was a simple gesture but an intimate one. She didn't like it or the little knowing smile on his mouth— or the way her heart jumped, when she felt his roughened fingertips brush her skin.

"Don't do that," she said, and jerked her head away.

"I could feel your eyes on me, when I was with the mare." He reached out again but she pulled back before he could touch her. "It made it tough to concentrate."

"All right, that's it. I should have done this yesterday. Kincaid, you're fired."

"For telling the truth?"

"Maybe you didn't hear me, cowboy. You are out of here! Collect your time from Abel and—"

She cried out as he caught her wrist and dragged her behind the bunkhouse. She swung at him with her free hand but he caught that wrist, too, pushed her back against the limestone wall and pinned her hands to her sides. Her heart thudded into her throat. His eyes had gone from green to black. He looked hard, and dangerous—and incredibly, savagely exciting.

"I'll scream," she said. Her voice trembled and he laughed softly. He knew, she thought, he knew she was as excited as she was terrified, and in that moment she didn't know which of them she hated more, Tyler Kincaid or herself.

"Does it frighten you, Caitlin?"

"Let go of me. Let go or so help me—"

"Wanting a man like me? Does it scare you, just a little?"

"Nothing scares me," she said, forcing her eyes to stay locked to his, telling herself that he couldn't hurt her, wouldn't hurt her, not here. The bunkhouse blocked them from view, yes, but they weren't alone, not really. There were men working only a few yards away. All she had to do was scream and this would all be nothing but a bad dream.

"Kincaid." Her lips felt parched. She ran the tip of her tongue over them. His gaze followed the motion of her tongue and the realization sent a hot, lancing need shooting through her. "Kincaid, look. This is a mistake. You must realize that. You can't get away with—with—"

His mouth twisted. "Is that what you think? That I'm going to rape you?" He laughed, though the sound of it was humorless. "Hell, lady, you think you've got me all figured out, don't you?"

"Just let go of me, dammit!"

"Answer a question first."

"You're not in a position to bargain, Kin—"

Her breath caught as he shifted his weight, moved just enough against her so that she could feel him—and, heaven help her, feel the heat of her own response slipping through her blood.

"One question," he said softly. He clasped both her wrists

in one hand and cupped her face with the other, tilting it to him. "Did you like watching me?"

She looked at him, told her pulse to stop its crazed race. "I told you, I wasn't—"

He bent his head, brushed his mouth against hers. "The truth," he whispered.

"No," she said, "no, I didn't. I—"

She caught her breath as he touched his mouth to hers again, rubbing his lips against hers, then nipping at her bottom lip. Scream, she told herself, scream and bring the men running...

He sucked her lip into his mouth, worried it gently with his teeth.

A moan rose in her throat. She tried to stop it but Tyler heard it, felt it pass from her lips to his, and he groaned, swept his arms around her, and kissed her.

CHAPTER FOUR

NOTHING in her life had prepared Caitlin for Tyler's kiss.

A first kiss between a man and a woman was supposed to be gentle, even cautious. How did his mouth feel against yours? How did your body fit in his arms?

That was how it was supposed to be.

Tyler's kiss wasn't like that.

His mouth was hot on hers, his arms hard as he gathered her to him and held her. She could feel herself being swept into a whirlpool of desire, and the sudden terror of giving herself up to it swept through her blood. Gasping, she tried to turn her face from Tyler's but he clasped it in his hands, brought his mouth to hers again…

And she was lost.

Lost, and drowning in the taste of him. The heat. The intoxicating scent of being possessed by an aroused male.

She moaned again and Tyler heard the sound and knew it marked her surrender.

Her arms wound around his neck and she lifted herself to him, fit her softness against the hardness of him. Tyler groaned, ran his hands down her back, down her spine, cupped her bottom and lifted her into the V of his legs, wanting her to know what she had done to him, that she had turned him from a civilized man into a creature that knew nothing but desire. Her touch, her taste, the feel of her in his arms, had reduced the world to this. He was blind to everything but the need thundering through his blood.

She moved against him, deliberately, provocatively. He felt the press of her breasts, the tilt of her hips. There was a roaring in his ears and he whispered her name, his voice low and rough, tugged her T-shirt out of her jeans, swept his hands up her back, along the warm silk of her skin.

She trembled in his arms.

"Tyler," she whispered against his mouth and just that, the sound of his name on her lips, drove the last shreds of sanity from him.

"Yes," he said, "yes, that's right. It's me, touching you. Me..."

His hand closed over her breast. She moaned, twisted against him to thrust the small, sweetly rounded flesh against his palm. His callused palm. His callused fingertips, fingertips that slid across the yearning, lace-covered nipple and turned her body to liquid honey.

"Please," she said brokenly, "Tyler, please..."

He groaned, thrust his hands down her jeans, his fingers cupping her backside, urging her to her toes, bringing her closer. Her nerves, her muscles, her heart throbbed with desire. Yes, she thought, oh, oh, yes...

"You son of a bitch!"

She heard the roar, felt the blow as it landed on Tyler's shoulder and reverberated through her body. Tyler grunted, Caitlin's eyes flew open, and she stared over his shoulder at the enraged face of her stepfather and the riding whip he brandished in his right hand.

Tyler's response was instantaneous. The tough kid he'd once been still lived inside him. He shoved Caitlin out of the way, spun around, lowered his head, raised his fists and struck his assailant. Jonas staggered back. He shook his head, snarled and came at Tyler again. But the red haze had cleared from Tyler's eyes, long enough to let him see that his attacker was an old man with a shock of white hair and a face that looked as if it had been seamed by all the winds in Texas.

"Hell," he said in disgust, and dropped his fists to his sides, "knock it off, Gramps. I can't fight an old man."

"Try me," Jonas said, and struck him again. It was Tyler who staggered this time, stunned not just by the blow but by the violence of the old man's attack.

This was ridiculous, he thought, and jerked back as the old-timer came at him again. What was he supposed to do? Stand here and get his tail whipped, or go down in history as the man who'd beaten Methuselah to a pulp?

"Put up your fists and fight," Jonas snarled. "I'm gonna whip your butt into next Sunday!"

"Stop it!" A slender woman with a cap of pale gold hair came running toward them. "Stop it this instant!"

"You stay out of this, Marta."

"She's right," Caitlin said fiercely. "Dammit, stop!"

Tyler held up his hands, palms out. "Look," he said reasonably, "this is crazy. I'm at least thirty years younger than you are—"

"More than that, I'd bet," Jonas said. "But if you think I give a damn about beatin' you up 'cause you're a baby, you'd better think again."

Tyler couldn't help it. He laughed, and the old man's pale blue eyes flashed with anger as he came at him.

"Hell," Tyler said wearily, and in a move so swift it was nothing but a blur, he caught the old guy's arm, jerked it behind his back and subdued him.

"Tyler." Caitlin looked around them and bit back a moan of despair. The fight had drawn a crowd. Men were gathered around, gaping the way they would at a bad accident on the highway. Nobody wanted to see the gory details but nobody wanted to miss them, either. She put her hand on Tyler's arm. "Please. Let him go."

Tyler flashed her a quick smile. My God, she thought, he's enjoying this.

"Kincaid." Her voice steadied. She lifted her chin and fixed him with the kind of look that had been known to make the toughest ranch hand tremble. "I said, let him go!"

"I heard you, McCord, but a man has to be a fool to let go of somebody who's determined to kill him."

"He's right," Jonas growled. "I *will* kill him, just as soon as I get loose."

"You see?" Tyler shot her that primal male smile again. "I let him go, he's going to come at me and then I'll be forced to beat the crap out of him." The smile changed, turned cold and dangerous, and he jerked back on Jonas's arm just enough to make the old man wince. "Your choice, mister. You want to waltz around like this another couple of hours, or are you going to tell me you'll behave?"

"Dammit, Kincaid!" Caitlin's voice was sharp with anger. "You said you came here to see Jonas Baron. Well, that's him you've got in an armlock."

Terrific, Tyler thought with disgust. If there was a better way to ensure that Baron wouldn't answer any of his questions, he couldn't imagine what it might be. He'd humiliated the old man in front of what looked like every hand who worked on Espada.

There had to be a right way to let go of a tiger, once you'd grabbed it by the tail.

"If you hadn't used some kind of pansy kung fu stuff on me," Jonas said, "you'd be hightailin' it into the next county by now."

Tyler grinned. "It wasn't kung fu, it was natural talent. Not that you're bad, for a man with one boot in the cemetery and the other in the hearse."

Someone in the little crowd laughed. Caitlin spun toward them, eyes flashing.

"Okay," she said, "that's it. Any man still here two seconds from now can collect his pay and get himself off Espada, pronto."

The men dispersed quickly, and she turned back to Tyler and her stepfather.

"You're behaving like children, the both of you."

Tyler gave her a look that said this had nothing to do with her.

"Look," he said to Jonas Baron, "I understand your distress. I'm sure it's, uh, difficult, coming on a scene like, well, like the scene you came on. Finding your stepdaughter in my arms must have been unsettling."

"In your arms?" Jonas snorted. "That's a nice way to put it. Truth is, if'n I hadn't come along to break things up, you'd have been up in the hayloft next."

"Dammit, Jonas!" Caitlin shoved her face at her stepfather's. "What you saw was none of your business."

"'Course it is. You're my daughter. No man wants to see his daughter bein' pawed."

"Oh, for heaven's sakes!" Caitlin stamped her foot in fury. "I am not your daughter, I'm your stepdaughter, as you have gone out of your way to remind me a hundred billion times in the last couple of years. And I wasn't being pawed. Hell, if anything, I was the one doing the pawing." She slapped her hands on her hips and glared at both men. "You know what?" she said in disgust. "You two deserve each other."

Tyler and Jonas both watched as the slender woman with the pale gold hair slipped an arm around Caitlin's waist. The women marched to the main house without looking back.

A moment passed, and then Jonas cleared his throat.

"All right," he said gruffly. "The girl spoke the truth. This is jes' plain dumb. You let go, I'll step back and we'll start from there. Deal?"

Tyler hesitated, then shrugged his shoulders. "Deal," he said, and let go.

Jonas grunted, rubbed the circulation back into his arm and looked at Tyler. A slow smile curled across his mouth.

"I got in a good shot there, across your cheek."

Tyler wiped a hand across his face, looked at the blood on his palm, then at Jonas.

"Yeah. And you're going to have black-and-blue marks for a month."

"Maybe."

The two men fell silent, then shot each other quick, grudging smiles, but Jonas's smile turned into a glower.

"You're Kincaid."

"Yes."

"Abel hired you?"

"Your stepdaughter did."

Jonas's pale eyes narrowed. "Did she, now."

Tyler smiled. It was a quick smile, the kind Jonas recognized from his own youth as the smile of a man as good with his head as he was with his hands.

"She hired me to work with the horses. I'm good at gentling the skittish ones."

The old man nodded. "I'll just bet you are." He bent down and picked up his hat. "Caitlin says you have business with me."

"I do." Tyler looked Jonas in the eye. "Important business."

Jonas nodded again. "Well, go get yourself cleaned up, then come on to the house and tell me what it is." His eyes swept over Tyler, taking in the scuffed boots, the faded jeans, torn shirt, bloodied cheek and cool, unreadable green eyes. "You look like a drifter and you might be good at gentlin' horses, Kincaid, but I get the feelin' that isn't what you do for a livin', nor is it what brung you to Espada."

Tyler flashed that hard, quick smile again.

"I'd heard you were a tough man, Baron, and a smart one. I don't usually put much store in secondhand information but it looks as if what I heard was right, on both counts. I'll see you in twenty minutes."

"Fifteen," Jonas replied, and headed for the house.

Twenty minutes later, Tyler knocked on the door—the front door—of the Baron house.

He'd showered, changed his jeans and shirt and brushed the dust off his boots. He'd never gone into a meeting as important as this one in anything but a suit and tie, but jeans were all he'd packed. Besides, he had the feeling confronting Jonas Baron in a suit would only make the stubborn old so-and-so think he had the advantage.

He smiled as the door swung open. "Carmen," he said pleasantly—but the woman in the doorway wasn't Carmen.

It was Caitlin.

She'd changed what she'd been wearing, too. No jeans, this time. She had on a blouse in a shade of pale pink that made him think of magnolia blossoms and a blue denim skirt. Her legs were long and bare, her toenails neat and unpolished in a pair of tan leather sandals. Her hair was wet, as if she'd just come out of the shower, and curled around her face in soft little tendrils. Her eyes were icy, her mouth unsmiling, but that didn't keep him from remembering how hot those hazel

eyes had been a little while ago, or what it had felt like when
he'd parted that pink mouth with the tip of his tongue.

Heat curled in his belly and he felt a flash of anger, at
himself and—even though he knew it was unreasonable—at
her. This was no time to let his anatomy do his thinking for
him.

His smile disappeared.

"I'm here to see the old man."

Caitlin raised an eyebrow. "Call him that to his face again
and you'll find yourself heading out the door quicker than you
came through it." She stuck out a hand as Tyler started past
her and poked a finger into his chest. "I want to be sure we
both understand what happened before, Kincaid."

"What's to understand?" Tyler said pleasantly. "You were
upset and angry. I caught you off guard, or maybe in a weak
moment, and that's the only reason you behaved the way you
did."

Her eyes widened. "Yes. But how did you—"

"How did I know you'd deny what really happened?" He
smiled coldly. "Trust me, McCord. It was easy."

"I'm sure there are women somewhere on this planet who
appreciate Neanderthals." Her voice was as chilly as his. "But
I can assure you, Mr. Kincaid, I am not one of them." She
stepped aside, motioned him in with an autocratic jerk of her
head. "My stepfather's waiting in the library. I'll show you
to it."

Tyler followed her down a long hallway. Her head was
high, her spine rigid; she was treating him as if they'd never
shared those mind-blowing kisses, as if she'd never moaned
as he cupped her breast.

Anger swept aside reason. He caught hold of her shoulder
and swung her to face him.

"Do you ever admit to having an honest emotion, lady?"

"All the time." She wrenched free of his hand and flashed
the kind of smile he figured Marie Antoinette must have
shown the crowd just before the blade of the guillotine
dropped. "I just did, in fact, but maybe it rolled right on past

you. I don't like you, Kincaid. In fact, I hope to hell I never see you again. Is that honest enough?''

"No." He looked at her mouth, his gaze lingering, then into her eyes. "It's not honest at all. We weren't talking about whether or not you liked me. Hell, McCord, if it comes to that, I don't like you much, either.''

He felt a rush of pure satisfaction to see her face turn pink but she held her ground, lifted her chin and looked straight back at him.

"You're right. I suppose I have to bear some responsibility for that—that unfortunate mistake down by the bunkhouse.''

"A mistake," he said, and she thought she heard a whisper of amusement in his voice. "Is that what you call it when you go crazy in a man's arms?''

"I did not go crazy," she snapped. "You're the one who's crazy, if you really think I—''

A door banged open somewhere down the hall.

"Caitlin? Girl, where the Sam Hill are you? And where in hell is that boy? He don't show up in the next minute, you tell him I've decided to forget about talkin' to him.''

"You want to see him," Caitlin said, "you'd better get a move on. Thanks to you, he's in a terrible mood.''

"You let me worry about Jonas Baron's mood.''

His tone was soft, the smile on his lips pure male arrogance as he reached out, cupped her chin and tilted her face up to his. Was he really going to try to kiss her? Anger rocketed through her—anger, and something else.

"Let go of me," she snarled.

"Have dinner with me Saturday evening and we can talk about which of us is crazy.''

"I'd sooner have dinner with an armadillo.''

"I'll pick you up at seven.''

"You show up at the door Saturday evening, the only thing you'll pick up is buckshot." Caitlin twisted against his hand. "Dammit, Kincaid, let go!''

Tyler laughed softly. "Seven. And don't be late. If there's one thing I admire, it's promptness in a woman.''

"You're unbelievable.''

"You see?" He flashed a grin so cocky it set her teeth on edge. "You just gave me a compliment, McCord. Our relationship is changing already."

"Caitlin?" Jonas's bellow roared through the hall. "Where are you? And where's that young fool thinks he can rough up an old man and get away with it?"

Caitlin pulled away from Tyler. Her heart seemed to have lodged in her throat and she tried to ignore its high, rapid beat.

"Dream on, Kincaid," she said, trying for a light tone.

Tyler's eyes darkened. He reached for her, pulled her into the curve of his arm, held her hard against him.

"That's a fine idea, McCord," he said softly. "I'll dream about what I want to do to you and you dream about what you'd like me to do. And Saturday night, we can make those dreams come true." He saw her eyes widen with shock, saw the sudden flutter of her pulse in the hollow of her throat just before he bent his head and kissed her. She made a little sound, just as she had the first time, and he parted her lips with the tip of his tongue. Her taste shot through his blood like a drug. For one wild moment, he wanted to back her against the wall, put his hand up her skirt, and take her right there, while the wildness beat inside him...

Dammit!

Tyler fought for control, let go of her and stepped back.

"Now," he said, as she swayed unsteadily, "you can show me to the library."

Her eyes flew open. She stared at him, her face flushed, and then she wiped the back of her hand across her mouth.

"I'd sooner show you to hell."

Her voice trembled and just before she turned her back to him, he thought he saw tears in her eyes. He almost reached out to her but what for? It was all illusion. It had to be. This was a game, that was all, and she played it well.

He followed her down the hall to a pair of massive, half-open doors. He could see Jonas Baron beyond them, standing in the center of a room crowded with ancient leather chairs and sofas, his dusty boots planted firmly on the delicately faded pinks and buffs of what had to be an Aubusson carpet.

"Mr. Kincaid is here," Caitlin said stiffly.

"And about time." Jonas jerked his head toward a mahogany sideboard. "Pour us some bourbon, girl."

"Pour it yourself," she said, and slammed the door on her way out.

Jonas chuckled. "My stepdaughter's not very happy with me jes' now." He eyed Tyler narrowly. "You look better, cleaned up."

"So do you," Tyler said politely.

The old man smiled, crossed the room to the sideboard and took out two crystal glasses and a bottle of bourbon.

"Twenty years old," he said, holding the bottle to the sunlight that streamed through the windows. "Slips down your gullet like silk." One bushy brow rose. "I s'pose you'd prefer somethin' else, boy. Beer, or wine, or maybe even some of that there colorless slop the Russkies drink."

"Actually," Tyler said, "I'm pretty much a bourbon man, myself." He held out his hand, took the drink Jonas poured him and smiled. "And if you call me 'boy' one more time, I'll have to deck you."

"I got three sons make the same threat all the time." He looked over the rim of his glass and frowned. "We meet before?"

"No." Tyler sipped his bourbon, gave a nod of satisfaction. "No, we haven't."

"Didn't think so. I may forget names, from time to time, but I never forget a face. Still, there's somethin' about you seems familiar. Where'd you say you was from?"

"I didn't."

Jonas sank down in a leather wing chair, motioned Tyler to sit across from him but Tyler shook his head.

"I'd rather stand."

"Suit yourself." Jonas reached for an elaborate humidor, opened it and held it out.

"Have a cigar, Kincaid. They're straight from Havana."

"Smuggled in?" Tyler said, and smiled. "Thanks, but I'll pass."

"You don't strike me as a man who'd pass up a good cigar 'cause it's illegal."

"I'm not." Tyler watched as Jonas bit off the end, spat it into a crystal ashtray, then lit up. "I just happen to think that putting an old boot in your mouth and lighting it up might taste better than smoking a cigar."

Jonas's eyes narrowed. He looked at Tyler, his mouth twitched and he laughed. "Not at all afeared of me, are you?"

"I've never met a man I've been afraid of."

"How about my stepdaughter?" Jonas took a puff on the cigar. "You afraid of her?"

"I'm not going to discuss your stepdaughter with you, Baron, except to tell you a man has to be a fool to put himself in a position where he has to be afraid of a woman."

Jonas grinned. "My philosophy, exactly. I've lived by it for years." He paused, looked at Tyler and frowned again. "You sure you and I ain't met before?"

"Positive."

"I jes' keep thinkin' you look like somebody I know. Kincaid, huh? You got a brother or a father I might have done business with?"

Tyler could feel the knot forming in his belly.

"It's possible you knew my father," he said carefully. "Perhaps that's why I look familiar."

"Mebbe." Jonas crossed his legs and looked up at him. "He a rancher?"

"I don't know."

"You don't know?" Jonas smiled. "What do you mean, you don't know? Your old man's occupation a family secret, or somethin'?"

Tyler took a deep breath. "I never knew my father. Or my mother, for that matter."

"Well, I'm sure that's tragic, Kincaid, but I can't see how it involves me." Jonas looked at the grandfather clock in the corner. "It's getting late. I have some phone calls to make."

"Amazing," Tyler said softly, "how that cowpoke accent of yours just disappeared."

The old man looked up, his pale eyes flat. "Amazing," he

said, just as softly, "how you're still here when I just dismissed you."

Tyler's teeth glinted in a humorless smile. "I don't 'dismiss' very well, Baron. In fact, I don't 'dismiss' at all."

Jonas got to his feet. "Maybe you need to be tossed out on your tailbone, boy."

"You're an old man," Tyler said quietly, "and I'd hate to hurt you but so help me, you put a hand on me again and you'll regret it."

Jonas stared into Tyler's eyes. A shudder seemed to ripple through his body and then he gave a curt nod.

"My wife would never forgive me if we bloodied up her precious rug." He folded his arms and smiled, the very picture of a man in control of himself and everything around him. "If you have a point to make, get to it."

Tyler lifted his glass to his lips, drank off the last of the bourbon. It went down his throat smoothly, just as silken in taste as Jonas Baron had promised, but it did nothing to ease the knot in his gut. He'd lived without knowing who he was—who John Smith was—for an entire lifetime. Why, suddenly, did it seem to matter so damned much?

"Kincaid? You got something to say, say it."

"You were right, when you said I wasn't what I seemed. I'm not a drifter, Baron. I'm not even a ranch hand. Not anymore." He put the glass down and looked at Jonas. "Did you ever hear of Kincaid Incorporated?"

"Finance? Land development, that sort of thing? Yeah, I might have. So what?"

"I'm that Kincaid."

"And you come walkin' onto my land, take a job wrasslin' stock?"

Tyler shrugged his shoulders. "It seemed like a good idea at the time. Now I'm offering my credentials so you won't think I'm crazy."

"Might think you're crazy anyways, you don't get to the point. Why are you here?"

Tyler tucked his hands into his pockets and began to walk slowly around the room, pausing every now and then to look at a painting or a bit of sculpture while he struggled for control. Finally he turned and looked at Jonas.

"I was born in Texas."

The old man stared at him. "Fascinatin'." He went to the sideboard and refilled his glass.

"In fact, I was born right here, on this ranch."

"On Espada?" Jonas lifted the glass to his mouth. Bourbon sluiced gently over the rim. "Well," he said, and barked out a laugh, "fancy that."

"But I don't know who gave birth to me, or who my father was."

"Uh-huh." Jonas took another drink. The glass trembled in his hand and he set it down, very carefully, on the sideboard. "As I said, this is all fascinatin' but it's got nothin' to do with me. I keep whelpin' records of calves and horses. The government takes care of everybody else."

Color striped Tyler's high cheekbones. Why in hell had he ever come here, or thought he could do this? He was not a man to talk about himself to anybody, and certainly not a man to bare the dark secrets of his past. And yet here he was, dumping the dirty little story of his birth at the feet of a man he'd disliked on sight.

"So," Jonas said, "is that it? I sure hope so, considerin' I got those calls to make."

"No," Tyler said sharply, "that's not it." Dammit, he'd come this far, made a fool of himself already. There was no sense in backing down now. "You had a couple of married men working for you, the year I was born. Their wives were pregnant."

"Their wives were—" The old man slowly exhaled. "I see. Well, I'll tell you what, Kincaid, I'd like to help you but I ain't never had a man named Kincaid workin' here."

"That wouldn't have been his name," Tyler said gruffly.

"Ah. Well, it don't matter. This would go back a piece, wouldn't it? Twenty-five, thirty years? And I don't have no recollection of—"

"Thirty-five years," Tyler said. "I was born on Espada, thirty-five years ago, on or about 18 July—"

Jonas stiffened. "July 18, you say?"

"Yes. And I was hoping…Baron?"

The glass fell from Jonas's hand and rolled across the carpet. Tyler reached him in two quick steps, caught hold of him and eased him into a chair.

"Baron," he said, looking down into the white face that suddenly looked every one of its eighty-six years, "don't move. I'll get help."

"Don't need help."

"Of course you—"

"Don't!" The old man reached out, clasped Tyler's wrist. His hand was clammy but his grip was firm. "It's just—it's the cigars, that's all. The cigars."

"You're sure?"

"Positive. I'm right as rain."

He didn't look right as rain, Tyler thought, and felt a whisper of guilt. In the past couple of hours, Tyler'd fought with a man old enough to be his grandfather, wrestled him into submission, interrogated him…

"No need to mention this to anybody," Jonas said gruffly.

"Sure. Whatever you say."

"Good. Good." Jonas rose to his feet. His color was coming back, and the hand he lay on Tyler's shoulder was steady. "Well, Kincaid, I wish I could help you, I truly do, but if there was men workin' for me all those years ago with wives with big bellies, I don't recall it."

Tyler nodded. In his heart, he'd expected as much. As for the feeling that there were secrets here, at Espada…if there were secrets, they were Baron secrets, and had nothing to do with him.

"It was just a shot in the dark," he said softly.

The men began walking to the door. "Glad to have met you," Jonas said, and grinned. "I'll bet this is the first time the head of a big company like yours got horse turds on his boots."

Tyler worked up a smile. "I had lots of horse turds on my boots, when I was a kid."

"Grew up on a ranch, did you?"

"For a while. It was a state home for boys."

"Did you, now?" Jonas looked at him. "Got yourself in some trouble, huh?"

"Some."

"So, that's where you learned about horses."

"Yeah." Tyler smiled again. "I was pretty good at it, too."

"Accordin' to my stepdaughter and my foreman, you still are." Jonas cleared his throat. "Did you ask Abel about these here big-bellied ladies supposed to have been on Espada, thirty years ago?"

"Thirty-five. No, no I didn't. I wanted to speak with you first."

"Well, don't you never mind, boy. I'll ask him. Ol' Abel's probably not gonna know nothin', either, but he's more likely to talk to me than to a stranger, jes' in case he does."

Tyler turned to the old man. "Thanks," he started to say, but the word caught in his throat. For the last few minutes, Jonas Baron had spoken pleasantly, his tone had been friendly, but now that he was looking into the old man's eyes, what he saw was the fiery glitter of hatred—or was it fear?

Tyler's own eyes narrowed. The old son of a bitch was conning him. Hell, he'd almost succeeded. Baron was hiding something instinct told him would lead to the truth about his birth.

"Somethin' wrong, Kincaid?"

Plenty, Tyler thought, but he smiled and shook his head.

"Not a thing," he said pleasantly. He put out his hand, sensed more than saw Baron force himself to take it. "Thank you for your help."

"No problem." Jonas pulled back his hand and stuck it into his pocket. "Bet you're goin' to head back to Georgia now, huh?"

Tyler waited a second before answering. "It's your bet, Baron. You put it on whatever horse you think will win."

The last thing he saw, as he walked out of the room, was the collapse of Jonas Baron's cocky, all-knowing smile.

The sight filled Tyler's heart with pleasure.

CHAPTER FIVE

CAITLIN stared at the library door after she'd slammed it behind her.

"The hell with the both of you," she muttered.

Tyler Kincaid and her stepfather deserved each other. They were both bullheaded, opinionated, arrogant jackasses. For all she knew, they might just end up squaring off again. This time, though, there'd be nobody to stop them.

Good, she thought grimly, as she walked toward the front door. Maybe they'd knock each other senseless.

Now, that was a pleasant prospect. She smiled, just contemplating it. It was what the two men deserved, Jonas for coming to her defense when she hadn't needed defending and humiliating her in the process; Tyler for thinking he could drag her into his arms and force his kisses on her in broad daylight while she struggled to shove him off her.

Caitlin stood still.

She had struggled, hadn't she? Of course she had. She'd fought like a wildcat. She hadn't wanted Tyler to kiss her or touch her, hadn't wanted his hands on her bare skin or his mouth, hot and open, on hers...

"Catie?"

Startled, she swung around. Her stepmother was standing at the entrance to the dining room, brows raised, a quizzical smile on her face.

"Marta." Caitlin took a deep breath and forced a smile to her lips, too. "I—I didn't realize you were standing there."

Marta cocked her head. "Has round two begun yet?"

"Round..." Caitlin laughed. "Jonas and Tyler Kincaid, you mean. Yes, I just showed Mr. Kincaid into the library."

"Ah. Well, I don't hear any thuds or grunts so far, so I

assume they're behaving themselves. I was just about to have some coffee. Won't you join me?''

Caitlin hesitated, then smiled. "I'd love to."

"Good." Marta linked her arm through her stepdaughter's and they walked slowly toward the solarium. "Are you all right? That was, um, it was an unfortunate scene that took place, down by the bunkhouse."

"Kincaid forcing himself on me, you mean," Caitlin said stiffly.

"Did he, really? From what little I saw, and from what Jonas said, I had the impression that what you and Mr. Kincaid were doing was mutually agreeable." Marta motioned Caitlin to a chair. "Perhaps I'm wrong."

Caitlin plopped down in the chair and stretched out her legs. "You're definitely wrong," she said, as Marta poured coffee. "Tyler Kincaid grabbed me and—and..." Her eyes met Marta's and she flushed. "All right. He kissed me, I kissed him back—but only because he caught me by surprise."

"Of course."

"What's that supposed to mean?"

"It means," Marta said mildly, "that I can understand how such a thing could happen. Your Mr. Kincaid is an extremely good-looking man. Some of Carmen's butter cookies, dear?"

"No," Caitlin said calmly, "thank you, but I don't want any cookies. And I don't want you jumping to conclusions, either. Tyler Kincaid is only good-looking if you like the type."

"I agree." Marta smiled into her coffee cup. "But what women wouldn't like that type? Tall, dark, gorgeous... I'm old enough to be your Mr. Kincaid's mother, dear, and I'm very happily married to your stepfather, but I can see why you're attracted to him. "

"Oh, for goodness' sake!" Caitlin put down her cup and saucer, hard enough so the delicate china rattled. "I am *not* attracted to him. I hardly know the man, and what little I do know, I don't like. And I wish you'd stop calling him that."

"Calling him what?"

"*My* Mr. Kincaid. All I did was give him a job."

"That's what I meant."

"He said he wanted to see Jonas. And he needed work."
Caitlin plucked a cookie from the platter and bit into it.
"You'd have done the same thing."

"Undoubtedly," Marta said gently.

"And on top of that, my horse got spooked and Kincaid
decided to play Galahad. I'm sure he thought he saved me
from getting hoofprints tattooed on my skull." She put the
rest of the cookie into her mouth and chewed it. "Well," she
said grudgingly, "maybe he did. The point is, I hired him on
and he did his job well—until today."

"When he forced his unwanted attentions on you."

"Yes. No. Oh, what's the difference? I'd have fired him,
too, if Jonas hadn't come along and made a scene."

"Jonas is very protective," Marta said softly. "He loves
you, Catie. You know that."

"You mean," Caitlin said tightly, "he loves me as much
as he can, considering that I'm not of his blood."

"I mean," her stepmother said, taking her hand, "that he's
stubborn and pigheaded. All the Baron men are, or do you
really think Slade, Travis and Gage are any better?"

Caitlin sighed. "No, you're right. They're all impossible.
Maybe it isn't a Baron trait. Maybe all men are like that. Just
look at how pigheaded Tyler Kincaid is—"

A crash echoed through the house. Both women jumped to
their feet.

"They're killing each other," Caitlin said.

"I think it was just a door slamming." Marta looked at
Caitlin. "But I do suspect Mr. Kincaid's meeting with your
stepfather is over."

"You get yourself off my property, Kincaid." Jonas's voice
roared through the house. "You got five minutes, you hear?
After that, I'll put some buckshot into your tail."

"Good," Caitlin said grimly. "Jonas fired him."

"Indeed." Marta sighed and put her arm around Caitlin.
"Will you excuse me, Catie? I think I'd better go remind your
stepfather that he's not supposed to get his blood pressure up
past the boiling point."

"Of course." Caitlin hesitated. "Marta?" she said, just as the older woman reached the door.

Her stepmother looked back at her. "Yes?"

"He is good-looking," she said softly. "Isn't he?"

Marta smiled. "If I were twenty years younger, I'd think about giving you some competition."

"Oh, I didn't... I wouldn't... I was talking hypothetically."

"Hypothetically," Marta said, and flashed a grin, "Mr. Kincaid is... I believe the current term is 'a hunk.'"

"Go tell Jonas to calm down," Caitlin said, and began to laugh.

Marta chuckled and hurried away. Still smiling, Caitlin circled the room, piling the coffee things on a tray, picking up another cookie, pausing to straighten the embroidered throw pillows on a love seat and, at last, almost as an afterthought, making her way to the window.

Yes, there he was, the all-powerful Tyler Kincaid, in full retreat.

Caitlin's head lifted. "No more Mr. Tough Guy now," she muttered, "are you, Kincaid?"

No sir, he certainly wasn't. He was hightailing it down the hill, the way men always did after Jonas Baron gave them a tongue-lashing...

Except, he wasn't.

Tyler was strolling down the hill. Hell, he was swaggering, shoulders easy, head high, hands tucked into his pockets. And he was in no hurry, despite Jonas's five-minute warning. He paused at the paddock, put one booted foot on the bottom rail and watched Manuel working one of the new horses. It seemed like a century rolled by before he stepped back, tucked his hands back into his pockets and made his way toward the bunkhouse.

"Idiot," Caitlin whispered.

What was he trying to prove? Not that she cared, one way or the other. Tyler Kincaid was none of her business. Did he really think his act would keep the men from knowing the truth, that Jonas had run him off?

She folded her arms, watching through narrowed eyes as he

climbed the steps to the door of the bunkhouse. Ten minutes from now, he'd be gone, and ten minutes later, he'd be forgotten. Hired hands came and went on Espada, and nobody so much as remembered their names.

Tyler Kincaid might think he was somebody special, but he wasn't. The men would forget him, she'd forget him...

She'd forget the way he'd kissed her, too. The way she'd felt when he'd touched her.

Caitlin's breath caught.

"Goodbye, Kincaid," she said firmly. Then she turned her back to the window, picked up the coffee tray and left the room.

The following week seemed interminable but at long last Friday slipped into Saturday, and there was at least a little time to relax.

By evening, Espada was quiet. Marta and Jonas had gone out to dinner. The men were either down at the bunkhouse, playing cards or watching TV, or in town, all duded up in pressed jeans and shirts, easing the work of the past days with the help of a couple of drinks and some much-wanted female companionship.

"Come to the Phillips's with us," Marta had said to Caitlin, but Caitlin had smiled, kissed her stepmother and told her, truthfully, that she was looking forward to taking a shower, putting on her sweats and curling up with a good book.

"Sounds like fun," Marta had said, but Jonas had glowered.

"Sounds like the girl's plannin' on bein' an old maid," he'd growled. "Give Leighton a call, why don't you? Bet he'd be happy to take you to the movies or maybe out for dinner."

"Leighton?" Caitlin and Marta had said in unison.

"Well, why not? He's your cousin, after all."

Caitlin hadn't been able to resist. "He isn't," she'd said primly, "he's a Baron."

"Exactly."

Marta had rolled her eyes. "Come along, Jonas," she'd said, and dragged him off while Caitlin tried to figure out what that had been all about.

She was still thinking about it as she stepped from the shower an hour later.

"Leighton," she said, and rolled her eyes the way her stepmother had done.

Better to spend the evening with a tarantula than with Leighton. She didn't like the man. Nobody did, even though he'd been trying to ooze charm ever since Travis, Slade and Gage had all married and made it clear that not a one of them wanted Espada.

"Looks like Jonas and I are the only Barons left in Texas," he'd said heartily, the last time he'd paid an unwanted visit.

Well, Leighton was kidding himself. Jonas had this idiotic bug in his head about leaving his land to a Baron but surely he'd never leave it to *that* Baron. Leighton's son, Gray, maybe, but Gray was off at some Eastern college, learning to be a lawyer. As for Leighton himself... Jonas wasn't a fool. He'd never leave his beloved Espada to a man who couldn't tell a steer from a bull, who'd cringe at the smell of good, honest-to-God horse manure.

Jonas was just trying to suggest she do something instead of staying home. That she'd even let herself think anything else only proved what a long week it had been. A skittish colt had kicked Manuel and broken his wrist; a freak hailstorm had done in the roof on the old barn and what should have been a simple trip to pick up a newly purchased stud turned into near-disaster when an eighteen-wheeler suddenly jackknifed ahead of the truck and horse trailer Caitlin was driving. She'd had to do some quick maneuvering to avoid plowing into it but she'd managed while Abel sat beside her, muttering epithets she'd never heard before—and she'd heard most everything, after spending so many years on a ranch.

Caitlin tossed the damp towel aside and ran her fingers through her hair.

But Jonas had been the real reason the week had been so awful. He'd been as snappish as a bear with a thorn in its paw ever since he'd had that meeting with Tyler Kincaid.

"Is something wrong?" Marta had asked him gently, just last night.

"Wrong?" he'd snarled. "Why do women plague a man with questions? Why should anything be wrong?"

And that, Caitlin thought as she opened her closet, that was a question in itself.

The things that had gone wrong this week were minor, when you came down to it. On a spread the size of this one, accidents were bound to happen. In fact, now that she reconsidered, it hadn't been such a bad week at all, except for Jonas's sour disposition.

Actually the week had been pretty good.

Tyler Kincaid was gone. Really gone. No last-minute attempts to confront Jonas again, or to see her. Well, why would he try to see her?

No reason. None at all. A good thing he hadn't, because she'd have refused to see him. The nerve of the man, to have sneaked himself into a job at Espada, just so he could try to sell Jonas some snake-oil proposition.

"Man wanted me to buy into a deal so full of holes I just laughed in his face, when he told me about it," was all Jonas would say, but it was enough.

Caitlin blew a curl off her forehead, pulled on a pale yellow sundress with skinny little straps and a full skirt. It was too hot to wear sweats, too hot to get her dander up, thinking about Kincaid and how he'd tried to make fools of her and her stepfather, too hot to do anything except go downstairs, pour herself a tall glass of iced tea, go out on the deck with the tea and her book and take it nice and easy for the rest of the evening.

She'd never have been able to do that if Kincaid was still here.

With him gone, she could sit outside without wondering if he was watching her. She could walk down to the stables without feeling the sudden rush of heat that meant his eyes were on her. She could forget about catching a glimpse of him gentling a horse, his voice as soft and husky as it had been when he was holding her, his hands as gentle...

"Oh, stop it," Caitlin said in disgust.

What was this nonsense? She was a woman, not a child.

And a woman didn't fantasize over a man just because he'd kissed her, especially when the memory of that kiss sent a hot lick of embarrassment rolling through her blood.

Caitlin picked up her comb and yanked it, hard, through her hair, wincing as she drove the teeth through the still-damp tangles. Then she stared at herself in the mirror.

She wasn't a pretty sight. No makeup. Hair that looked as if it had been arranged by Little Orphan Annie's stylist. Well, so what? She didn't have to worry about how she looked.

There was nobody here to see her. Nobody who mattered, now that Tyler Kincaid was—

Caitlin swore, tossed the comb aside, pulled her hair back low on her neck and secured it with a rubber band. Carmen would be wondering what was taking her so long. She'd asked her to fix her something to eat more than an hour ago.

"Enchiladas, maybe," she'd said hopefully, and Carmen had said, *sí*, enchiladas it would be...

"But a young woman should not spend Saturday night by herself."

It was an old speech, abbreviated over the years to that one pithy line. Caitlin's response varied, depending on the circumstances. This time she'd fallen back on an old standard.

"Esme should hear you say that," she'd said, and smiled teasingly.

Carmen had not smiled in return. "Just because my daughter is foolish enough to be a women's lubber is no reason for you to be the same," she'd grumbled, and Caitlin had laughed and hugged her.

"It's women's lib, not lub. And Esme isn't one, she's just smart enough to know a bright woman can be perfectly happy without a man to mess things up."

"Exactly," Caitlin said to her reflected image.

Then she opened the bedroom door and clattered down the stairs, to the kitchen.

The house was quiet.

Caitlin paused at the foot of the steps. Well, no. It wasn't. She could hear sounds. Voices, coming from the kitchen.

The TV set? No. She recognized Carmen's laugh, sliding over the deeper laughter of a man.

A man, huh?

Caitlin grinned, tucked her hands into her pockets and headed toward the back of the house.

Another peal of laughter rang out. "Oh, *señor*," Carmen said. The words held a girlish lilt belying Carmen's years.

Caitlin's grin broadened. She'd stroll in, hang around just long enough to collect her supper and give Carmen's suitor the once-over, and then she'd make a fast exit.

"You are too kind, *señor*," Carmen said, just as Caitlin stepped into the room.

"Carmen," she said gently, "I can see that you're definitely not a women's lub..." The teasing words died as the housekeeper swung toward her—the housekeeper, and Tyler Kincaid.

"Good evening, Ms. McCord."

Answer him, Caitlin told herself. Say "good evening," or "hello," or, better still, say, "Mr. Kincaid, you just get your tail out of this house." But she couldn't seem to get herself together long enough to manage anything that might even approximate a logical sentence because the sight of him simply stole her breath away.

If he'd been gorgeous before, in faded jeans and a T-shirt, he was spectacular in light tan chinos, an open-necked white dress shirt and a tweed sports jacket. She'd thought of him a thousand times during the week—what was the harm in admitting it, so long as she admitted it only to herself? She'd even dreamed about him, dreams that she didn't like to think about once daylight came. And yet, even in those dreams, she'd somehow managed to forget that Tyler wasn't just handsome, he was gorgeous.

The line from a country and western ballad whispered in her ear. Tyler Kincaid was as easy on the eyes as he'd be hard on the heart...

"Cat got your tongue, Ms. McCord?"

He was laughing at her. She could see the little glints of amusement in his eyes. Even Carmen, the traitor, was smiling, as if Caitlin had stumbled on some wonderful prize hidden inside a *piñata*.

"Mr. Kincaid." Caitlin drew herself up. "Mr. Kincaid, at the risk of sounding like a bad cliché, what are you doing here?"

"Why, Ms. McCord, I'm disappointed." He regarded her steadily, his expression polite. "Have you forgotten our date?"

"Our...?" Caitlin put her hands on her hips. Really, the man was impossible. "We have no date."

"Of course we do. Saturday night? Dinner?" He frowned, glanced at his watch, which was either the real thing or the best Rolex imitation she'd ever seen. "I have to admit, I couldn't recall whether we'd agreed on a time but I figured, well, seven-thirty would be just about right." He raised his eyes to hers. "You look beautiful."

The compliment was the kind a man like him would toss out all the time, but it made her feel giddy. And that, in turn, made her angry.

"Do you really think you can—you can just march in here and get your own way?"

He grinned. "She's not very hospitable," he said to Carmen, "is she?"

"She is surprised, *señor,*" Carmen said politely, "that is all."

It wasn't all, not by a long shot. The housekeeper flashed Caitlin a look and reminded her, in a staccato burst of Spanish, that she had been raised to have better manners. Caitlin thought about pointing out that Tyler Kincaid, for all his good looks, didn't seem to let a thing like good manners stop him from going after what he wanted, but the smile on his face told her he was enjoying the performance and she wasn't about to prolong it for his benefit.

"I can see you've made a convert of Carmen, Mr. Kincaid, but that's just because she doesn't know you as well as I do."

The housekeeper threw up her hands and stalked from the room. Caitlin headed in the opposite direction.

"I'll see you out."

She heard his footsteps as he fell in behind her. Was it really going to be this easy? she thought…and got her answer when she opened the front door and he reached out and shut it.

"Dammit," she said, swinging toward him, "must I draw you a picture? My stepfather will have you drawn and quartered, if he finds you here."

Tyler grinned. "Really."

"Yes, really. Honestly, Kincaid—"

"Honestly, McCord, it's getting late. Do you need a wrap? If you do, get it, please, and let's go."

"Do you have a hearing problem, Kincaid? We are not having dinner. Not together, anyway."

"You disappoint me," he said softly. "I didn't think you were afraid to cross your stepfather."

"Afraid? Me?" She snorted. "Don't be ridiculous. You want to talk about being afraid of Jonas, mister, let's talk about you."

Tyler laughed. Well, why wouldn't he? What a dumb thing to have said, she told herself furiously. He'd never be afraid of any man, or of anything.

"I guess you can hear my knees knocking, huh?"

"Go ahead, laugh. You won't be laughing when I call down to the bunkhouse and have some of the men throw you out."

"Don't," he said. He was still smiling, but his eyes had turned cool. "They're a nice bunch of guys. I'd hate to have to hurt any of them."

Caitlin opened her mouth, then shut it. She'd been on the verge of telling him how conceited that sounded, but he was probably right. No one would be able to stop him, if he set his mind to something.

"Look," she said, "this is silly. You were told to pack your gear and go."

"I left because there was no further reason for me to stay."

Caitlin couldn't hold back her surprise. "But Jonas said—"

"Whatever story he told you was a lie. I came to see him. Well, I saw him, and I left." A smile angled across his mouth. "And now I'm back for our date."

"We don't have a date."

"Of course we do. I asked you to have dinner with me tonight."

"And I turned you down."

"Are you afraid of me, McCord?"

Caitlin looked at Tyler. He was smiling again, but there was something in his eyes that made her heartbeat quicken. Yes, she thought, yes, I am afraid of you. Of what you made me feel, when you touched me. Of what I might feel again...

"Cait?"

No one ever called her that. The name sounded strange— but it sounded right, as if it were something special between them, a shining new link that bore his imprint.

Her heart stuttered again. Stop it, she told herself. Stop being such a fool.

"No," she said coolly, "of course not."

"Have dinner with me, then."

"I already said I wouldn't, Kincaid. What's the sense of making this into some childish game, where you dare me, and I double-dare you..."

She fell silent as he closed the distance between them.

"Take the dare," he said softly. He looked at her mouth, and she could feel her lips part as if he'd run his finger over them.

"Kincaid..."

"My name is Tyler." He reached out, threaded his hand into her hair. The rubber band came loose and he pulled it free. Her hair felt just as he'd remembered, like fluid silk against his skin. "Say my name, Cait."

"Tyler." Her tongue felt thick. "Tyler, please. You have to leave."

He clasped her face in his hand, bent his head and kissed her. His mouth was hot and hungry and she moaned softly before she twisted her face away.

"Caitlin." He brought her face to his, tilted it so their eyes met. "I want you," he said roughly. "In my arms. In my bed."

"Don't," she said breathlessly. "Please. Don't say things like that."

"I thought of you all week, of how it would feel to taste your skin, to be inside you."

His words were raw, and so were the images they conjured. She saw herself lying in his arms, saw him kneeling between her thighs, felt him touching her.

Caitlin began to tremble. Push him away, she told herself. Hit him. Kick him. Do all those clever things you were telling yourself you should have done when he kissed you that last time...

He kissed her. It was a kiss she knew a man might give a woman as she lay beneath him. He slipped his tongue between her lips, moved it against hers, drew her close so she could feel the heat and the hardness of his aroused flesh.

A moan broke from her throat. The room seemed to spin; they were at its center, caught in a whirling kaleidoscope of colors.

"Cait," he whispered, and cupped her breast.

She felt her heart beating against his palm .

"Cait," he said again, and this time she looked up into Tyler's face. What she saw there was exciting. Incredibly exciting. His green eyes were so dark they were almost black, and filled with the promise of the pleasure he would bring her if she went to bed with him...

If she went to bed with him? With this stranger, who'd come onto Espada and into her life as if he were one of the conquistadors who'd invaded this land in centuries past, claiming both it and her for his own?

Caitlin wrenched free of Tyler's embrace.

"I'm sure that macho performance holds appeal for some women, Kincaid." Her blood was still pounding in her temples but her voice was icy. She lifted her chin and fixed him with the kind of look that would make even old Abel take notice. "But I am not 'some women.' I don't like to be mauled, or told what to do, and if you came here tonight thinking I was going to fall at your feet in a swoon, you're in for a disappointment."

He looked back at her in silence, his expression unchanging

except for a tiny muscle that knotted and unknotted in his cheek.

"Hell," he said, with a little smile, "I think I'd have been more disappointed if you had."

Was he giving up that easily? Not that she was sorry. Of course, she wasn't sorry. Caitlin smiled politely and stepped back.

"In that case, Kincaid—"

"In that case, McCord," he said, and before she could shriek or scream or even protest, he scooped her off the floor, tossed her over his shoulder and headed into the night.

CHAPTER SIX

CAITLIN got her voice back, but by then it was too late. Tyler had already carried her down the steps, to his car.

"Kincaid," she shouted, "are you nuts?"

"Probably."

He sounded amused, damn him. Amused, while she dangled over his shoulder, facedown, like a sack of laundry.

"Put me down," she demanded, pounding her fists against his back. "Damn you, Kincaid, put—me—down!"

"Your wish is my command," Tyler said, and dumped her into the leather seat of something big and expensive-looking. A Land Rover? A Navigator? As if it mattered, she thought, blowing the hair out of her eyes. As if it really, honestly, for-a-minute made a difference if you were kidnapped by a man who drove an ultrapricey Sports Utility Vehicle when he hadn't even had wheels a few days ago.

She made a lunge for the door. Tyler, already behind the wheel, pulled her back and buckled her seat belt, dodging her flailing hands, then giving a nod of satisfaction when he had her trapped and trussed like a chicken ready for the roasting pan.

"Okay," he said, and turned the key. The engine roared to life. He put it in gear, let out the clutch and the SUV sped down the gravel road that led away from the house.

"I am not a fan of macho behavior," she said coldly.

"How about barbecue?" Tyler's hands flexed on the wheel. "You a fan of that?"

Caitlin blinked and looked at him. "A fan of…?"

"Barbecue. Ribs so sweet, they melt in your mouth. Sweet potato pie. Pulled pork." He heaved an exaggerated sigh of pleasure. "Fantastic. But if you'd rather have Pacific Rim—"

"Pacific…?"

81

"Rim. Hasn't it reached Texas? It's food with an Asian feel. Not Chinese, not Japanese—"

"I know what Pacific Rim cuisine is, Kincaid." Maybe he really was nuts. Maybe it made sense to treat him with care.

"In that case, which do you prefer?"

He smiled politely, as if he hadn't just kidnapped her from her own home, hadn't just kissed her until she'd thought her bones would melt.

"You have to tell me, Cait. So I can phone ahead and make the arrangements."

"The arrangements," she repeated foolishly. Maybe he wasn't crazy. Maybe she was.

"Uh-huh. I didn't know which you'd prefer, Barbecue or Pacific—"

"—Rim."

"Right. So I have them both on standby."

Caitlin imagined every barbecue joint in the state of Georgia, every restaurant on the Asian continent, waiting eagerly for Tyler's phone call. She bit back a hysterical laugh.

"You're wasting your time, Kincaid."

"Caitlin," he said, as if she were six instead of twenty-six, "let's not make this into a full-blown war. I'm hungry. You must be, too. Carmen said you hadn't eaten since noon."

"Carmen," she said icily, "talks too much."

"Just pick one, okay? Pacific Rim, or—"

"I know how this works, Kincaid. You give me choices, narrow ones, but choices just the same. And I'm supposed to see that as an act of kindness, and that's supposed to make me form an emotional bond to my captor."

He laughed. Really laughed, and all at once the outrageous silliness of the whole thing hit her and she wanted to laugh, too.

Instead she folded her arms and stared out the window.

"If you were a Texan," she said, each word bearing a coating of ice, "you'd know how ridiculous that question is. Barbecue, of course."

Tyler grinned, took out his portable phone and punched a button. "Get out those ribs," he said.

Then he stepped harder on the gas and the SUV flew into the night.

She was angry.

Tyler took his eyes off the road just long enough to take a fast look at Caitlin.

Angry didn't do it. Angry was the understatement of the century. From the set of her jaw and the rigidity of her posture, he was pretty sure that "furious" was a much better bet.

And he couldn't much blame her.

He'd come on to her with all the subtlety of an octopus, told her he wanted to take her to bed, and while she was still trying to come to terms with that, he'd picked her up, tossed her over his shoulder like a sack of dirty linens and walked off with her.

He shifted in his seat.

Well, not exactly. He'd never describe Caitlin McCord as a sack of laundry, not with all those soft curves. She was all woman, every inch of her—and if he didn't stop thinking that way and get his mind back on the winding, dark road, they were going to end up a statistic.

"—a date?"

He looked at Caitlin again. She was staring fixedly at the road ahead, her arms still folded across her chest and her chin up so high he wondered if she could see out the window.

Damn, she was beautiful.

"I asked you a question, Mr. Kincaid. Is this the way you normally get a date?"

She certainly had a point there. What in hell had gotten into him?

"And if it is, do you ever wonder why the woman in question is always busy when you ask her out again?"

Dammit, what *had* gotten into him? He'd asked her out the day he'd had his confrontation with Baron. No. No, that wasn't quite accurate. He hadn't "asked" her, he'd told her. What difference did it make? The bottom line was that he'd shown up tonight, knowing she'd never agree to spend the evening with him.

"Dragging a woman into your cave by her hair may go over well wherever it is you come from but somebody should have warned you that it's frowned upon here."

"Okay, you've made your point." Tyler looked at her. "I don't normally drag my women off by their hair."

"I am not 'your' woman."

"Not yet."

Caitlin decided not to rise to the challenge, the same as she decided to ignore the little shiver of excitement his words sent zinging down her spine.

"Look, if I came on a little strong…"

"A little strong? You came on like a tank, Kincaid. And I don't like it."

"Really? You could have fooled me." He looked at her again. Her face was difficult to read in the muted glow of the dashboard lights. Still, he thought he could see the rise of color in her cheeks.

"Ditch the sarcasm, Kincaid. It doesn't work."

"It wasn't sarcasm, baby, it was the truth. You want me as much as I want you. And I've wanted you since the moment you damn near rode me down with your horse."

She swallowed dryly, put her hands in her lap and folded them tightly together.

"Well, here's another truth, Kincaid. You're wasting your evening."

Tyler gave a soft laugh. "Really."

"I have no intention of—of sleeping with you."

"I'm glad to hear it, because I have no intention of sleeping with you, either." His voice roughened. "When I take you to bed, sleep will be the last thing either of us will do."

"My God, you're insufferable! You're so damned sure of yourself!" He heard the angry hiss of her breath, then the rustle of her skirt as she sat up even straighter. "I hope you enjoy your evening, Mr. Kincaid, because I promise you, it will be the last one you spend in my company."

Tyler smiled. "When you know me better, Ms. McCord, you'll know that it's always a mistake to offer me a challenge."

"And when you know *me* better, you'll know that wasn't a challenge, it was a promise."

"Call it whatever you like." He glanced in his mirror, turned on a signal light, and swung onto a narrow, unlit road. "What I heard was a challenge."

"This is a really stupid conversation," Caitlin said coldly, though her thoughts were anything but cool. The road was endless, easily as long as the one leading to Espada. Tree branches whipped by overhead, blocking out the moon. Where was he taking her? She knew every inch of this country. There wasn't a restaurant within miles.

All at once, lights studded the darkness ahead. She sat forward and focused on the dim outline of a building.

"Is this place new? I know just about every barbecue pit in Texas," she said warily. "And I've never heard of one out here, in the middle of nowhere."

She could see the building clearly now, in the glare of the headlights. It was long and low, and if it was a restaurant, it certainly wasn't doing very much advertising. There was no sign out front, no parking lot...

No other cars.

Caitlin swung toward Tyler.

"Okay, that's it." Her eyes narrowed as she looked at him. "Take me home."

"Certainly."

He pulled up before the building and shut off the engine. Night sounds crowded around them, the buzz of a billion insects, the keening yip of a coyote.

"Kincaid." Stay calm, she told herself. Stay calm, sound as if you're not afraid, and he'll take you home. Tyler Kincaid might be an enigma, but he wasn't a barbarian. "I want to go home."

"You *are* home." He stepped from the car, went around to her side and opened the door. "Well, to be specific, you're at my home."

She jerked away when he reached for her but he caught her hand and linked his fingers through hers.

"Cait," he said softly, "I live here."

Her gaze flew to his. "Here? But when I asked Jonas, he said—"

She clamped her lips together, but it was too late. The words were already out of her mouth, he'd heard them, and the look on his face told her what a mistake she'd made.

"You asked your stepfather about me?"

"No. Of course not. Well, yes. I mean, you and he obviously had a row, and then you left, and I—and I…" Dammit! The more she said, the worse it sounded. She took a deep breath and stepped from the car. "All right," she said briskly. "I admit, I was curious."

"Aren't you curious now?" He jerked his chin toward the enormous house behind them. "I am, if you're not. I saw this place for the first time this morning."

"You what?"

"I asked the realtor to show me some ranch property. She took me to half a dozen places but when I saw this one, I knew it was right." He grinned. "At least, I think it's right. It comes furnished."

"How nice for you," she said lamely.

"Yeah, that's what I thought. So—I put a deposit on it but I'd like an honest opinion before I sign the papers tomorrow."

"An honest opinion." Caitlin cleared her throat. "That's why you brought me out here? To ask me what I think of this house before you buy it?"

"Sure. What do I know about Texas ranches? I'm just a Georgia country boy, myself."

She looked at him through narrowed eyes. Tyler Kincaid was as much a country boy as she was the queen.

"Cait? Do me a favor. Take a look."

He wasn't a man who asked favors of anybody, either. There was something wrong with this entire setup…but damn, she was curious. And now that she'd taken a better look at the house, that curiosity was growing.

"Is this the Wilson place?"

Tyler nodded. "Do you know them?"

"No. Well, not exactly. I came here with Jonas once, when Charlie Wilson was raising money for his Senate run." She sighed, tugged her hand free of Tyler's and stepped from the car. "I don't know what I can possibly tell you that the realtor couldn't."

Tyler led the way to the front door. "Well," he said, as he opened it and turned on the lights, "for starters, you can tell me if there's some law that says those things have to hang at the windows."

Caitlin stared at what looked like yards and yards of deep crimson, scalloped and fringed and festooned with heavy gold fringe.

A laugh bubbled up in her throat. She bit it back and took a quick look around her. Not just crimson drapes and gold trim, but cupids and shepherdesses and naked cherubs, too.

"I'd heard that Charlie's second wife had the place re-done," she said, and then she couldn't help it. She snorted, snorted again, and hooted with laughter. "Oh my gosh, it's awful!"

Tyler breathed a sigh of relief. "You can't imagine how relieved I am to hear you say that. The realtor—"

"Who is she?"

"Lady name of Pru Barnes. Do you know her?"

"Oh, yes. I certainly do. The woman acts as if she has a stick up…" Caitlin colored. "She's stiff-necked. Folks lay bets on what will happen, the first time she smiles."

"Yeah, well, she's not gonna smile around me, I can tell you that." He crossed the room and tugged at the drapes. "I told her the place looked like a world-class bordello. For a minute, I thought she was going to faint dead away."

Caitlin threw back her head and laughed. "I love it! I just wish I'd been here to see… Kincaid? Kincaid, what are you…"

Tyler gave a last wrench and the drapes fell to the floor in an undulating sea of crimson.

"I asked for your opinion," he said innocently, "and you gave it. Goodbye, drapes."

Caitlin grinned and reached for a cherub. "Goodbye, cherub?" she asked, nodding toward the enormous fieldstone fireplace that ran half the length of one wall.

Tyler folded his arms. "By all means."

He watched as her hand closed around the ugly little figure's fat bottom. She turned toward the fireplace and looked at it. The tip of her tongue—such a pink, delicate tongue—stuck out between her teeth.

"Really?" she said, glancing at him again.

"Really."

Caitlin drew back her arm and hurled the cupid onto the hearth.

"Wow," she said, whirling toward him. Her cheeks were flushed, her eyes were bright, and he wanted to take her in his arms and kiss her so badly that he felt the ache right through his bones.

But he didn't move, didn't touch her. Instead he smiled and brought his hand to his forehead in a lazy salute.

"Nice throw."

She smiled. "I was taught by the best."

Tyler lifted an eyebrow. "Nolan Ryan?"

Her smiled broadened. "Gage Baron. My middle step-brother. I was ten when I came to live on Espada, and the last thing Gage or Travis or Slade wanted was a girl underfoot."

"But they got to know you, and to like you?"

"What they got was tired to death of seeing my face. I guess they decided the only way to handle me was to take me into Los Lobos."

"Their baseball team?"

"Their gang. The Los Lobos pack. They made me a member after my mother took off for New York—" She broke off, looked at him and flushed. "I don't know why I'm telling you the story of my life," she said stiffly, "when what you asked for was my opinion of those drapes."

"I'm glad you are," he said softly. "I want to know more about you."

And I want to know everything about you.

The words were so clear in her mind that for a second, she thought she'd spoken them aloud. But she hadn't. Of course, she hadn't. She'd never say anything so foolish to any man.

"And I," she said, with a quick little smile, "want to know more about this house. Why did you decide to buy it?"

Tyler's smile tilted. "Land is a good investment."

"Ranching can be a lousy investment. You're at the mercy of the weather, the market—"

"I can afford it."

She liked the way he said it, with no false modesty and no arrogance. "I figured that. And that makes it all the harder to understand why you came to Espada the way you did."

"I wanted to talk to your stepfather, and to check on some things."

"Things you thought you'd learn more about if nobody knew you were rich?"

"Yeah." He shrugged. "Something like that."

Caitlin nodded. "You play things close to the vest, Mr. Kincaid."

"As do you, Ms. McCord."

They smiled at each other, and then his smile slipped. "Caitlin..."

"Show me the rest of the house," she said quickly, and before he could answer, she walked rapidly around the living room, pausing to shake her head over a china figure or to roll her eyes at a painting.

"The second Mrs. Wilson seems to have had a thing for, ah, for plump naked ladies and big horses."

Tyler laughed. "I said something like that to Ms. Barnes."

"You didn't."

"I did."

Caitlin grinned. "Better watch out, Kincaid. Pru will take her commission, then come after you and try and wash out your mouth with a bar of soap." She moved on, her smile fading, and paused at a bronze sculpture of a man mounted on a horse. "Oh, this is beautiful," she said softly.

Tyler watched her run her hand over the bronze. "Yeah." He cleared his throat. "I have the next piece in the series in my house in Atlanta."

"A Remington?" Caitlin looked at him and smiled. "A real one, numbered and signed like this?"

"Yeah." He shrugged his shoulders, foolishly pleased she should recognize the piece that was, in fact, the pride and joy of his Georgia collection. "So, what do you think? Do you like the house?"

Caitlin laughed and whirled in a circle. The skirt of her yellow sundress flared around her knees. She was more beautiful than the bronze, Tyler thought, and felt his belly tighten.

"I love it! It's a wonderful house, or it will be, after you get rid of all the froufrou. Can't you see this place done in pale oak?" She swung toward him. "In soft southwestern col—"

"What's the matter?"

Tyler was what was the matter. While she'd been talking, he'd slipped off his jacket and rolled back his cuffs. And oh, he was so beautiful. She'd never imagined using that word to describe a man, but what other word was there that would work? That strong-boned face. The thick, dark hair, and the little whorl of it visible in the hollow of his throat. Those powerful wrists and muscled forearms...

Yes, he was beautiful, far more beautiful than the Remington. And he wasn't unyielding bronze, either. He was muscle and bone, warm skin and hot mouth...

"So," she said brightly, as she turned her back to his suddenly knowing eyes, "you bought the Wilson place, Remington and all."

"Yes." His voice was low. The rough sound of it kicked her pulse into overdrive.

"Well." She gave a tinkling laugh, the sound painfully artificial even to her own ears. "I guess this makes it definite. You're not a drifter, are you, Mr. Kincaid?"

"Caitlin."

She closed her eyes as he came up behind her. She could feel the heat of his body and when he put his hands on her shoulders and drew her back against him, she knew she couldn't go on hiding behind bad jokes, or cold words, or an anger she no longer felt.

"Don't," she said, in a shaky whisper. "Please, don't. I'm not—I'm not ready to deal with this, Tyler."

His fingers pressed into her naked flesh as he turned her toward him. She looked into his eyes and it was like standing at the edge of a precipice, when logic assures you that you're not going to fall but something dark and deep within urges you to jump.

He put his hand under her chin and she lifted her head. Don't, she thought, but her lips parted...

Tyler brushed his mouth gently over hers.

"I'll go see to dinner," he whispered.

"Dinner," she said, with a quick smile. "Don't tell me you hired a cook."

"'Billy's Bar-B-Que Take-Out,'" he replied, smiling back at her. "'You Call, We Haul.'"

She laughed, grateful for the reprieve...and caught her breath as Tyler pulled her into his arms and kissed her, not gently, not as if she were made of glass, but as if he were going to take her, right here, right now, and heaven help her, she wanted him to, wanted him to...

"Find us some wineglasses," he said softly, as he put her from him. "And then why don't you come and join me in the kitchen?"

"Sure," she said brightly.

Just as soon as she was sure she could walk on legs that had the consistency of jelly.

They dined on the patio, at a candlelit table with the starry sky for a canopy.

They ate their barbecued beef on translucent china, buttered ears of corn with sterling silver butter knives, drank a soft, wonderful red wine from plastic glasses.

"Plastic glasses?" Tyler said, when Caitlin produced them, and she laughed and shrugged her shoulders.

"Maybe Mrs. Wilson thought they went with the cupids and the drapes."

Plastic or no, the wine was wonderful. So was the barbecued beef.

"Wonderful," Caitlin said, smiling at Tyler over the last of the wine.

He grinned. "I'll be sure and tell Billy you said so."

Caitlin touched her fingertip to a drop of barbecue sauce left in her plate, then licked it off. Tyler's smile tilted as he followed the simple action.

"So, what do you do? In Atlanta, I mean."

He shrugged and leaned back in his chair. "This and that."

"Ever the mystery man, huh?"

"I'm no mystery man, Cait. You can look me up in Dun and Bradstreet anytime you like."

"Will Dun and Bradstreet tell me why you sneaked onto Espada?"

The smile fell from his lips. "I thought we settled that. I told you, I wanted to talk to Jonas. And—"

"And check things out. Yes, so you said. That still doesn't explain why you showed up on our land, looking like a drifter."

"Our land? Do you have a share of Espada?"

"No." Caitlin's mouth thinned. "I think I told you, I'm not a Baron."

"And only Barons are good enough to own Espada?"

"Something like that."

"But you love the ranch. And you damned near run it."

"Yes, and yes…and please don't try to change the subject. Why did you come to Espada?"

Tyler looked across the table at this woman he'd only met days ago. There was no artifice to her, neither in the way she looked and dressed nor in the way she spoke. He'd known so many women in his life…some of them must have had more perfect features, more voluptuous bodies. He knew, for certain, that he'd never dined on Texas ribs at a table set outside a handsome house all done up like an overblown whore.

He knew, too, that he'd never spent a more wonderful evening, that he'd never dreamed he'd hear a woman tell him she wasn't ready for what they both wanted and know, in his gut, he wasn't ready, either, because he was flat-out scared of what she made him feel.

And he knew that this was the first time in his thirty-five years he'd ever been tempted to tell a woman the truth. To say, look, I know this is going to sound crazy, but I don't know who I am. I don't even know my real name. That's why I came to Espada, to try to solve the mystery that's haunted me all my life...

Was he losing his mind? Tell her that he was an orphan? That he'd grown up first in the care of two polite people who'd never particularly cared for him, then in the even more tender care of the state? Tell her that he'd spent the better part of a year at a place for kids who'd gotten themselves in trouble?

He pushed back his chair and got to his feet.

"Tyler, please." Caitlin rose, too. "Tell me what's going on. Jonas has done nothing but growl since he threw you out."

"Threw me out?" He gave a snort of laughter. "It would take that old son of a bitch and his three sons to throw me out, and even then, they'd have a tough time doing it. Besides, I didn't bring you here to talk about Jonas Baron."

"Tyler, if you'd just listen..."

"I am listening." He came around the table toward her, his eyes locked on hers. "I liked the way you said that."

"Said what?" Caitlin cleared her throat and took a step back. "What did I say?"

"My name." She caught her breath as he reached out his hand and touched her cheek. "Say it again."

"You're right," she said unsteadily. "It really is late..."

"Caitlin."

His voice was as soft as honey but there was a roughness to it that sent a lick of flame through her blood. He was so beautiful. So impossibly, dangerously male. He was everything a woman would dream of, everything *she* had dreamed of since she'd first begun to wonder what it would be like to lie in a man's arms and give herself up to passion.

"Tyler," she whispered, and she knew that one, softly spoken word had given everything away. His green eyes darkened and his gaze fell to her mouth. She trembled as he reached for her, as she imagined his weight bearing her down into the softness of his bed.

"I'm on fire for you," he said huskily, and kissed her.

She didn't fight him. How could she, when the taste of his mouth was richer than wine? When the feel of his arms was everything that mattered? She moaned as his tongue parted her lips, and she arched against him and wound her arms around his neck.

Tyler swept his hands down Caitlin's body, molding her, marking her with his touch. He groaned, slid his hands up under her skirt, and it was almost his undoing. God, how he wanted her.

"Sweet Cait," he whispered, and he cupped her bottom, lifted her to him, shuddering when she pressed herself against him. "Come to bed with me," he said, against her throat. "Let me make love to you until dawn lights the sky."

Caitlin moaned and tore her mouth from Tyler's. She pressed her face to his throat and inhaled his scent.

"I—I don't do this," she whispered. "I don't."

Tyler drew back, cupped her face, and lifted it to his.

"Damned right, you don't, " he said fiercely. "You're only going to do it with me."

She struggled to hold on to reason. Things were moving too quickly. She knew what she'd always believed was right and what was wrong, but Tyler had swept all of that aside. Right and wrong had given way to hunger and need, and it frightened her.

"I need—I need time," she said. "We just met. You hardly know me, and I don't know anything except that you're Tyler Kincaid."

The change in him was stunning. He let go of her and stepped back, his eyes cold and flat.

"And that's not enough, is it?" His voice was quiet but she sensed the fury of the storm beneath the calm façade. "After all, who in hell is Tyler Kincaid?"

"No. That isn't what I meant."

"Of course it is. And you're right to ask the question. A woman would be a fool to get involved with a man who has nothing but a name."

"I don't understand what you're talking about."

He walked across the room and stood looking out at the dark hills. Seconds passed. When he turned to her again, she felt as if she were looking at a man wearing a mask.

"It's late, Caitlin, and we've both had a long week." He smiled as he came toward her but the smile was empty of meaning. "I'll drive you home."

His hand closed on her elbow. His touch was polite and removed. It was hard to believe that only moments ago, his touch had seared her with fire.

"Tyler." She touched his shoulder. "Please, what's wrong? I didn't mean to upset you."

"It's all right," he said gently. "You didn't."

He gave her the same empty smile as he had before, pressed his lips lightly to her forehead and took her back home, to Espada.

CHAPTER SEVEN

MARTA was waiting at the foot of the steps when Caitlin came down the next morning.

She shook her head before Caitlin could greet her, put a finger to her lips and drew her aside.

"What's wrong?" Caitlin asked, lowering her voice to a whisper.

"I just wanted to warn you that Jonas is in a terrible mood this morning."

"As if that were something new. He's been mean as a rattlesnake all week."

"Yes, Catie, but I have the feeling you're going to be the one getting all his attention."

Caitlin blew out a breath in exasperation. "What'd I do to get so lucky? Near as I can tell, I followed every one of the orders he snarled at me."

Marta sighed and took her stepdaughter's hand. "It's about last night."

"What about last night? He wanted me to be sure and remind Abel to check on that colt, and I did."

"No, no, dear, this has nothing to do with the ranch." Marta cleared her throat. "Were you out with Mr. Kincaid last evening?"

Color rose in Caitlin's cheeks. "Marta," she said stiffly, "you know how much I care for you, but I really don't think—"

"You don't think who you see is any of my business, and you're right, of course. It's Jonas. He heard about your date—"

"It was hardly a date. Mr. Kincaid showed up here without any warning. I went with him so I could make sure he understood that I have no intention of ever seeing him again."

96

Marta said nothing but she didn't have to. The look on her face said it all, and who could blame her? Caitlin thought irritably. The excuse sounded laughable, even to her.

"Anyway, I don't owe Jonas an explanation." She tugged her hand free of Marta's but not before giving her stepmother's fingers a reassuring squeeze. "I think there are times he forgets that I'm a grown woman."

"I know he does." Marta smiled. "As far as my husband is concerned, you're still his little girl."

"Not his," Caitlin said stiffly. "Never his. I'm not a Baron, remember?"

"Oh, Catie, I know he's hurt you terribly by saying you can't inherit Espada, but—"

"You've got it wrong. He won't *let* me inherit Espada. There's a big difference. And it's crazy. He trusts me to run the ranch, to oversee everything that goes on here, but because I don't carry the precious Baron blood, I'm not good enough to—" Caitlin broke off the rush of angry words and threw her arms around her stepmother. "Oh, Marta, I'm sorry! He's your husband and you love him."

"And you love him, too, Catie."

"I do, dammit, despite the fact that he doesn't love me. Not the way he should."

Marta stepped out of Caitlin's embrace and clasped her shoulders.

"He loves you with all his heart. And he's proud of you. He talks about you to everybody." She sighed. "Trouble is, he's as stubborn as a mule when it comes to Espada. He built this place from nothing, you know that. Fifty acres of dirt, a secondhand tractor, two horses—"

"And a dozen head of cattle." Caitlin had to smile. She'd heard the story a thousand times but never grown weary of it. "I know." She sighed, kissed Marta on the cheek, then smiled at her. "Really, I do. And if I try hard, I can even see things from Jonas's viewpoint. He created a kingdom and he wants to bequeath it to someone who carries his blood." Her chin lifted. "But for all of that, I still think he's as stubborn as a mule."

Marta grinned and put her arm around her stepdaughter's waist. The women started slowly toward the dining room.

"An excellent description," she said. "I might just have trouble looking at my beloved husband from now on without seeing him with a pair of twitching ears."

The women looked at each other and burst out laughing.

"Glad somebody's in a good mood this mornin'," a deep voice grumbled.

Caitlin looked up. Her stepfather was seated in a high-backed chair at the head of the massive dining-room table, his bushy brows drawn together. The king, holding court, she thought grimly, and tried her best to see the picture Marta had painted with words—Jonas with a pair of twitching mule ears—but it was difficult to manage. Difficult, hell. It was impossible.

No mule could ever look so coldly furious.

"Jonas," Marta said, the word a gentle plea, but Caitlin looked at her and shook her head.

"It's okay," she said softly.

Marta sighed, gave her a quick hug, and hurried away. Caitlin waited a moment, until she was certain she had her temper under control. Then she walked to the sideboard and poured herself a cup of coffee.

"That's all you're gonna have for breakfast?"

She smiled pleasantly at her stepfather as she sat down at the table. "And good morning to you, too," she said.

"Ain't nothin' good about this mornin'." Jonas reached for a platter of biscuits and shoved them toward her. "Nothin' good about goin' around with an empty belly, neither. Eat somethin', girl."

"I'm not hungry, thank you."

"Et too much last night, did ya?"

The first shot had been fired. Not that she was surprised. Jonas wasn't noted for his subtlety.

"What's the matter?" She looked over the rim of her cup and smiled politely. "Didn't your spies fill you in on the menu?"

She was gratified to see two streaks of color arch across his cheekbones.

"Carmen ain't a spy. She's jes' interested in your welfare."

Jonas bent over his plate and attacked his bacon and eggs with more energy than was warranted. Behind him, the kitchen door swung open just long enough for Caitlin to see Carmen shake her head from side to side and roll her eyes. Caitlin nodded. The housekeeper's message was clear. However she'd divulged the information about Tyler's visit, it had been done innocently.

"Well?"

Caitlin jerked her attention back to her stepfather. He'd pushed aside his plate and was glaring at her over the oversize coffee mug he favored.

"Well, what?"

"Don't you gimme no sass, girl." He banged the mug down on the table. "You got an explanation for what you done, I'm ready to listen to it."

"Explanation? Sass? Girl?" Caitlin put down her cup, too. "Is there someone else in this room, Jonas? Some child you think you can address like that?" Her eyes grew as chilly as his. "There must be, because you surely wouldn't speak this way to me."

The old man stared at her. His mouth narrowed, then twitched, and finally he grinned.

"You're a chip off the old block, missy. There are times listenin' to you is like listenin' to a younger version of me."

"Not enough of a chip, evidently," Caitlin said coolly, "but let's not get into that, this morning." She rose, went to the sideboard and refilled her cup. "Yes, Tyler Kincaid came here last night. Yes, I went out with him. Yes, we had dinner, and—just to save you the trouble of asking—yes, I suspect he'll ask me out again."

"And? When he does, what'll you say?"

"I'll say, yes." Yes? Where had that come from? Until the word left Caitlin's lips, she'd have been willing to swear she would never agree to see Tyler again.

'Dammit!" Jonas slammed his fist against the table. "You

listen to me, Catie. That man is up to no good. No good whatsoever."

"How do you know that?"

"I just do, that's all. He came sneaking onto Espada, pretending to be something he wasn't—"

"I'm sure he had his reasons." What in hell was she doing, defending Tyler, especially since she'd made the same accusation just last night?

"Never mind that. I do not want you seeing him again."

"Why not?"

Jonas glared at her. "I don't have to explain myself to you, girl. You're not to see the man again. Is that clear?"

"What's clear," Caitlin said coolly, "is that you've managed to lose that down-home accent of yours again. How *do* you Barons manage that, I wonder?"

Jonas kicked back his chair and stood up. "Did you hear me? You're not to see Kincaid again."

Caitlin's jaw firmed. Her stepfather towered over her, but neither his temper nor his size had ever been enough to make her back off in a confrontation with him and she wasn't about to start backing off now.

"I'd have to be deaf not to hear you!"

"Just make sure you do as you're told."

"You can't order me around, Jonas."

"I can and I will."

"No, you cannot!" She stood, slapped her hands on her hips and jerked her chin up. "I'm not a child."

"Well, you're behaving like one! Letting that man suck up to you—"

"Oh, for heaven's sake! Why would he suck up to me? I'm nobody. I have nothing he could possibly want." Her eyes narrowed. "Tyler Kincaid's got more money than God, Jonas. Did you know that?"

"Money isn't everything."

"No. No, it certainly isn't. I'm just taking your remark to its natural conclusion. You obviously think Tyler's interested in me because he thinks I have money, and I'm telling you he doesn't need anybody's money, much less what little I've got.''

"You can have all the money you want, girl. Have I ever denied you anything?''

"Dammit,'' she said angrily, ''that's not what I'm talking about and you know it. You said Tyler wants something I've got, and I said—''

"I heard what you said.'' Jonas tucked his hands into his back pockets. ''Maybe he wants something other than money.''

"Maybe.'' Caitlin flushed. ''In which case, I'm perfectly capable of deciding for myself whether or not to let him have it.''

"You got a smart mouth on you, young lady.''

"I'm sorry you think so.'' Caitlin pushed her chair toward the table. ''Now, if you'll excuse me—''

"I wasn't referring to sex.''

She looked at him. ''What?''

"When I said maybe he wants something other than money, although I'm sure the son of a bitch wants that, too.'' Jonas took a deep breath. ''I was referring to Espada.''

Espada. Everything always came down to Espada in Jonas Baron's world. Caitlin gave him a brilliant smile.

"Ah. Now I get it. Tyler wants to get his hands on the ranch.''

"Maybe.''

"The man's a megamillionaire, he lives a thousand miles from here, he never heard of us and we never heard of him but he wakes up one morning and says to himself, 'Kincaid, you know what I want? I want something only Jonas Baron can give me.'''

Jonas looked at her for a long moment. Then he picked up his mug and turned to the sideboard.

Caitlin laughed. ''I hate to burst this bubble, but Tyler's already bought himself a ranch. The Wilson spread. You remember it, don't you? Big, handsome house. A couple of thousand acres of prime pasture and woodland. Not the size of Espada, I'll admit, but I suspect it'll do.'' She stared at her stepfather's straight back, muttered a curse and started for the door. "I have news for you, Jonas. Not everybody thinks owning Espada is the most important thing in the world."

"I do. And so do you."

The cruel words stopped her in her tracks. She took a breath before swinging around. Jonas was looking at her, his face expressionless.

"Is that what this is about? You think Tyler's sniffing around me because he thinks I stand to inherit Espada?"

Jonas folded his arms over his chest. "It wouldn't be the first time a man's tried to get at what he wants through a woman."

"Well, not to worry. You and I both know Espada will never be mine. If it makes you feel better, I've told him that already."

"You told him that? That you weren't going to inherit the ranch?"

"Not in those words, no." She flashed a brittle smile. "I just made it clear I'm not one of the anointed."

"You're sure of that, are you?"

"That Tyler's not interested in me because he thinks your little kingdom will be my dowry?"

"That you're not—what did you call it?—one of the anointed. If there's one thing life's taught me, girl, it's that things change."

Caitlin had never been at a loss for words in her life. Now, she was. All she seemed able to do was stare at her stepfather's impassive face.

"Did you hear what I said, Catie?"

"I—I heard you." She swallowed dryly. "But I don't know what you're talking about."

"Let me put it in plain English. What I'm talkin' about is that I'm not sure you won't inherit Espada."

"But you always said—"

"I know what I said, that I'd only leave this ranch to someone who carries Baron blood." Jonas's eyes turned flinty. "Best of all worlds, that would still be what I want. But my sons have made it clear they have no intention of coming back

2

to live on Espada, and I didn't build this spread to be run by some stranger they hire after a gravestone holds me down.''

''Jonas.'' Caitlin reached out a hand toward him, her voice softening. ''You're a long way from that. We don't need to talk about this now. For all you know, Trav or Slade or Gage will come around.''

The old man snorted and gently batted her hand away. ''That ain't gonna happen, and you know it. And even if I live to be a hundred, I want to draw my last breath knowin' I've left this land in good hands.'' That same icy look came into his eyes again. ''What I'm sayin' is that it's finally dawned on me that blood isn't always a good thing.''

Caitlin blinked. ''It isn't?''

''Ain't that what I jes' said? No, it isn't. I never thought about it before but there are times it can be a bad thing.''

''Blood can be a bad thing?''

''Damnation, girl, will you stop soundin' like a parrot?'' Jonas reached into his breast pocket, took out a cigar and rolled it between his fingers. ''Here's the bottom line, Catie. I've been doin' some thinkin'. And, I don't know, maybe— maybe you're the right one to inherit Espada, after all.''

Caitlin pulled out a chair and sank into it. ''You're serious,'' she said softly, ''aren't you?''

''I am.'' Her stepfather put the unlit cigar between his teeth and bit down on it. ''But I haven't made my mind up yet, so don't you go getting' any bids on the north slope timber.''

''No,'' she said, and managed a quick smile, ''I won't.''

''I need to, ah, to sort some things out, before I reach a decision. And to talk with my boys, of course.''

''Of course.'' Was it possible? Had Jonas finally realized her passion for Espada matched his? That she would cherish the land, nurture it, as he had ? That she would see to it that his name, and Espada's, were never forgotten?

''Meanwhile, you steer clear of that Tyler Kincaid.''

Caitlin came to her feet. ''You old SOB,'' she said softly. ''So that's what this is all about! You think you can dangle the ranch in front of me to keep me from seeing him?''

''No. Hell, no! I just want to protect you.''

"You just want to protect Espada." Caitlin fought back the bitter taste of Jonas's cruel attempt at manipulation. "I don't know why you hate him so much."

"I told you. He's a liar. A cheat. He's up to no good, after something that isn't his."

"He's after me," Caitlin said, jabbing a finger into the middle of her chest. "Me, Jonas, not your precious ranch." Her voice wobbled and she cleared her throat. "I'm the attraction for him, not you. And I'll tell you something else, while I'm at it. I was going to refuse to see him again."

"But a few minutes ago, when I asked you, you said—"

"I said it because you made me so damned angry by trying to interfere."

It wasn't true, and she knew it. She'd said she'd see Tyler again because she wanted to, because she'd tossed and turned all night, imagining what would have happened if she hadn't stopped him from making love to her.

But none of that was Jonas's business.

Caitlin tossed her hair back from her flushed face.

"Well, now you've made me even madder. So I'm going to go out with Tyler Kincaid as often as he asks me. Every night of the week, if he likes. Hell, if he doesn't ask me out, I'll ask him." She glared at Jonas. "Stick that into your pipe and smoke it," she shot over her shoulder, as she made for the door.

"Catie, dammit, don't you walk out on me!" Jonas lunged after her, caught her wrist and turned her toward him. "Little girl," he said in a wheedling tone, "little girl, I'm only interested in what's best for you."

"Bull spit," she snarled, wrenching her hand free of his.

"My Lord, you didn't take on like this when I asked you not to go out with that snake, Leighton."

"Last evening, you were telling me to call him up!"

"You know I didn't mean it, Catie." Jonas's mouth twitched. "Compared to Leighton, a snake's good company."

"Damned right. He wants this ranch so badly there's nothing he wouldn't do to get it." Caitlin's eyes narrowed. "But I tell you right now, Jonas, if you'd tried this same trick, if you'd dangled Espada in front of me and tried to convince me *not* to date him, I'd have run into his arms so fast it would have made your head spin.''

"You're just talking to hear yourself talk, girl. You'd never play up to that slimy nephew of mine. Why, Leighton is a—"

"Did I hear my name mentioned?"

Caitlin and Jonas turned at the sound of the hesitant voice. Leighton Baron stood in the doorway, an oily smile on his face.

"Leighton," Caitlin said. She flashed a look at her stepfather, then strolled to Leighton's side. "You did," she said, and looped her arm through his. "Jonas was saying how long it is since you stopped by." She smiled. "And I said it surely was, and that I'd missed seeing you. Have you been away?"

Leighton looked from Caitlin to Jonas, and then at Caitlin again.

"Why, ah, why, no. No, I haven't." He put his hand over hers and Caitlin fought back a shudder of revulsion. "What a charming reception, my dear."

"Catie." Jonas's voice was low and heavy with warning. "Catie, don't be a fool, girl. You remember what I said about—about the future."

Caitlin gave a trilling laugh. "The future," she said. "Who cares about the future? I think people should live in the present. What do you think, Leighton?"

Leighton hesitated. Caitlin could almost see the wheels turning in his head as he tried to figure out which way the wind was blowing.

"Uh, well, I, ah, I think there's merit to both convictions."

"What you think there's merit to," Jonas said with a lazy smile, "is not ever sayin' nothin' that might put you on my bad side. Ain't that right, nephew?"

Leighton's Adam's apple bobbed as he swallowed. "If I seem to defer to you, Uncle, it's only because you're so wise."

Oh, yuck, Caitlin thought, but she gave him a big smile. "You should have been a diplomat, Leighton, you're so good with words."

Leighton beamed. "Thank you, my dear. Actually I did think about going into government service once, but—"

"But Washington decided there was enough hot air blowin' around without your help," Jonas said, and took the cigar out of his mouth. "You come by for some reason, or was it just to make sure my day would get off to a bad start?"

Leighton cleared his throat. "Actually," he said, "actually…"

"Were you going to invite me to brunch?" Caitlin said sweetly.

"Damnation," Jonas roared. "Girl, are you crazy?"

She was. She had to be. Tarantulas were the only things creepier than Jonas's nephew and when you came down to it, she really didn't have anything against tarantulas. They were big and ugly but they were honest, unpresupposing creatures, and they worked hard for a living. Leighton, on the other hand, was tall and good-looking, but he was as deceitful as the beauty in the eye of a hurricane, and he'd never worked a day in his life, thanks to the oil leases his father had left him.

Leighton wouldn't know a callus from a cauliflower, she thought scornfully. He wasn't anything like Tyler. She had the feeling Tyler had worked hard for what he had. It had left him with a man's hands, callused, not soft. With a man's muscles and body. Such a hard, beautiful body…

"Leighton?" she said briskly. "Did you want to take me to brunch, or didn't you?"

"Catie." Jonas's words barely concealed the steel in his voice. "I want you here today."

Beads of sweat popped out on Leighton's forehead. "Jonas wants you here today," he mumbled.

Like hell he did, Caitlin thought. She turned to Leighton and put her hands on his shoulders.

"Why, Leighton, I'm disappointed. I thought it was *you* who wanted me!"

Leighton shot Jonas a quick, helpless look. "I do. Of course, I do. I mean… I'd love to take you to brunch, Catie, but Jonas just said—"

"Who cares what Jonas said." Caitlin smiled into

Leighton's eyes. "Oh, come on, Leighton. We'll have such fun. Don't you want to have a good time with me today, hmm?"

"Why don't you answer her, Leighton? Don't you want to have a good time with our sweet Caitlin?"

Caitlin saw the color drain from Leighton's face. She made herself move slowly as she dropped her hands from his shoulders and turned around.

Tyler stood in the doorway, a picture of raw male power. He was dressed much as he had been the first time she'd seen him, in a snug T-shirt, faded jeans and boots, but the resemblance ended there. Today, his face might have been carved from granite, his eyes from green glass. He stood with his feet slightly apart, his hands deceptively loose at his sides. There was a presence to him that made her heart leap into her throat.

She thought of the magnificent sculpture she'd seen last night. That was what Tyler reminded her of: a tall, dangerous outlaw out of the Old West, come to life.

"Tyler," she said again, and he looked at her, his eyes so cold she almost shuddered. "Tyler, we—we weren't expecting you."

"So it would seem."

She heard Leighton make an unintelligible sound as he took a step backward. Jonas—Jonas just stood there, staring at Tyler.

My God, Caitlin thought, what was happening here? Leighton was scared out of his skin. Well, that wasn't much of a surprise. A man like Tyler would always scare the life out of the Leightons of this world. But Jonas—Jonas wasn't doing anything. He wasn't telling Tyler to get out of his house, or cursing, or even opening his mouth.

And she wasn't doing much better. A minute ago, she'd been on the verge of babbling an explanation of why she'd seemed to be in Leighton's arms. For what reason? Tyler was nothing to her. She was sure Jonas was wrong, that Tyler hadn't come on to her because of Espada, but he had lied his way onto the land and into her life. And he'd sure as hell not been a gentleman last night, literally carrying her off...

Seducing her, and almost succeeding.

Caitlin's breathing quickened.

Tyler Kincaid was dangerous. That was why Jonas and Leighton were afraid of him, but she was the one with the most to fear. He wore jeans and boots, rode horses, pitched hay—but for all of that, he came from another world and he would surely return to it, when he tired of Texas and her.

What an interesting diversion she must be for a man like Tyler Kincaid. She could picture him in his thousand-dollar suits, in a Lamborghini or a Porsche, and she could picture his women, too, women who smelled of perfume, not of horses. Who wore silk, not denim. Whose fingernails were long and polished, not short and often nicked...

Women who'd know how to play his games, without having their hearts broken.

Tyler took a step forward.

"Caitlin," he said softly, his eyes never leaving her face. The word was a statement, a question, and she prayed he couldn't see the pulse leap in her throat as she turned blindly to Leighton and wrapped her hand around his arm.

"This is Leighton Baron," she said. "Leighton, this is Tyler Kincaid."

Leighton moistened his lips, hesitated, then put out his hand. It trembled. Tyler looked at it but didn't take it.

"Another Baron," he said, with a predatory smile. "How nice."

"Leighton and I were just going to brunch."

"No." The word burst from Leighton's throat. "I mean— I mean..." He smiled nervously. "We thought we would, but now that company's come, well, obviously—"

"What are you doing here, Kincaid?"

Every eye turned to Jonas. He'd drawn himself up and moved forward. His posture, his bearing, even the jut of his jaw, seemed a duplicate of Tyler's.

"My stepdaughter's not going to see you again, so you might as well turn around and make for the door."

Tyler looked at Caitlin. "Is that right?" he said softly. "Have you decided not to see me again?"

Caitlin's throat constricted. "No. I mean—I mean, yes. That's what I decided." She moved closer to Leighton. "There's nothing here for you, Kincaid."

Tyler smiled, that same chilling smile he'd given Leighton only moments before.

"You're mistaken," he said, and looked at Jonas. "We have business, old man."

"We finished our business, Kincaid," he said brusquely. "And I told you to get off my land."

"You told me you figured I had no reason to hang around, Baron. But you were wrong. Very wrong." Tyler jerked his head in the direction of the library. "You want to talk about what happened thirty-five years ago man-to-man or right here, with your stepdaughter and your nephew standing by?"

The color drained from Jonas's normally ruddy face.

"Jonas?" Caitlin moistened her lips. "Jonas, shall I send for some of the men?"

"It's all right, Catie." Jonas managed a twisted smile. "Mr. Kincaid seems to think we have somethin' to discuss. Well, seein' as how it's a Sunday and I have nothin' on my schedule, I might as well oblige him."

Jonas seemed to gather himself together. Caitlin stared after him as he left the room. Then she let go of Leighton's arm and walked toward Tyler.

"I don't know what you're up to, but he's an old man. And your presence upsets him."

Tyler gave a mirthless laugh. "I'll bet it does."

"I want you out of this house, Kincaid."

"This has nothing to do with you."

"You're wrong. If it concerns Jonas, it concerns me."

"Dammit, Cait—"

"My name is Caitlin," she said, jerking back from his outstretched hand. "You just turn around, walk straight out the door and get the hell off Espada."

Tyler looked from her to Leighton. "What'd you say your name was, pal?"

"Leighton." Leighton's voice shook. "Leighton Baron."

"Well, Leighton Baron, Ms. McCord seems a bit upset.

Why don't you take her out, the way you'd planned, and feed her a good meal?''

"Oh, no. I mean, I wasn't really—''

"Sure, you were.'' Tyler smiled lazily and reached out for Caitlin. She tried to step back but he curled his hand around the nape of her neck. "You take her to have brunch, but you bring her straight back.'' He looked into Caitlin's eyes, and her heart skipped a beat at what she saw blazing in his. "And then,'' he said, his gaze never leaving hers, "then, you turn around and forget you ever knew her because Caitlin McCord belongs to me.''

"No,'' Caitlin said, but it was too late. Tyler drew her to him and crushed her mouth under his.

She struggled, beat her fists against his chest…and then she moaned, opened her mouth to his and kissed him back.

CHAPTER EIGHT

KISSING her had been a mistake.

Tyler knew as much, as soon as he drew Caitlin into his arms. The boy he'd once been might have done something as brash and aggressive but the man he'd become would not.

That man wore custom-made suits and chaired board meetings. He was civilized and urbane, and took pride in being a lover who always brought a woman pleasure but never, ever lost control. Even at the most explosive moment of sexual release, a part of that man always remained removed.

He told himself that part of him was still there, that he was kissing Caitlin only because the contemptuous way she'd treated him today infuriated him, after the way she'd melted in his arms last night.

It had nothing to do with wanting the taste of her on his lips. He was observing the kiss more than experiencing it.

And then her mouth—her hot, sweet mouth—opened to let him in, and he was lost.

Everything was lost. Common sense, reality—there was just Caitlin, soft and eager in his arms. He forgot where he was and who he was; forgot that they were not alone. He was caught in a whirlpool and he couldn't escape, didn't want to escape. He was being drawn down and down into its raging heart.

He clasped her face in his hands, angled his mouth over hers again in hungry need. She whimpered, lifted her hands and grasped his shirt. And then, just as suddenly, he felt her stiffen and she wrenched her mouth from his.

"Don't," she said, in a shaky whisper.

Don't. That was what she'd said. Not, "How dare you?" or "Let go of me," not some stock phrase that would have

111

meant she was determined to lay the blame for what had just happened on him.

Instead she'd whispered that one word, and when he opened his eyes and looked down into her beautiful face, his heart turned over. Her eyes were wide and liquid; her mouth trembled. The truth was there, painted on her every feature. She was afraid, not of him but of what he felt, what *she* felt, the same blood-hot need to take each other, to give everything and refuse nothing.

It was the last thing he'd ever wanted to feel about a woman, the last thing he wanted to deal with now.

And yet—and yet, it was there, had been there from the first time he'd touched her. The burning need to possess her. The longing to carry her off to some private place, tear off her clothes and sink deep into her welcoming flesh. There'd be no tenderness, not the first time. But after they were both sated, he'd do all the things he dreamed of doing to her. He'd kiss every inch of her skin, inhale her flowerlike scent. Touch her breasts, her thighs, the delicate inner petals that were hidden between them. Watch her eyes fill with pleasure, swallow her sighs...

Reality caught up, punched the breath from him like a fist to the belly.

For God's sake, man!

What was he doing? Had he lost his sanity? Maybe. A man had to be nuts to stand in the Baron foyer and make love to the stepdaughter of the man he now knew always had been, and always would be, his enemy.

And he'd done it all with an audience.

The guy with the smarmy smile was still standing there, tucked into a corner as if he hoped nobody would notice him, only now his eyes were the size of saucers.

"Let go of me, Kincaid."

He blinked, looked at Caitlin. Carefully, deliberately, he took his hands from her.

"I'm sorry," he said quietly, but he could tell, from the look she gave him, that "sorry" wasn't going to do it. Her eyes weren't dark with passion now, they were hot with anger.

"You'll do anything to embarrass me, won't you?"

"No. Hell, no. I didn't kiss you to—"

"Leighton?" Caitlin's cheeks were still pink, but her composure was back. "Leighton," she said again, without looking away from Tyler, "where are you?"

Leighton, Tyler thought wryly, had gone from a man trying to squeeze into a corner to one trying to merge with a wall.

"Leave him out of this," he said softly. "It's not his affair."

Wasn't it? Caitlin wasn't sure. For all she knew, Tyler had kissed her for Leighton's benefit. To put his brand on her. To defeat her, maybe even to try to control her. He wanted something, something that had to do with Jonas and Espada.

And he was dangerous to her.

Every instinct warned her Jonas was right, that Tyler was trying to use her as a tool in some far larger plan—but it all flew out of her head when she was in his arms. Even now, when he wasn't touching her, she could hear the roar of blood in her ears. The way he was looking into her eyes, his gaze so private and watchful. The shape of his mouth, and the knowledge of how it had felt against hers...

Yes. He was dangerous, but if he reached for her again, she might—she might—

Help me, Caitlin pleaded desperately of whatever gods might be listening, *help me, please.*

"Leighton." Years of dealing with Jonas had made her a hell of a good actress. Her tone was cool and steady, tinged with an unmistakable ring of authority. "Are you going to let this—this stranger insult me?"

Tyler sighed. "Ah, Caitlin, Caitlin," he said, almost mournfully.

She stepped back. "Leighton?"

"I'm here, Caitlin." Leighton sounded so pathetic that she almost—*almost*—regretted involving him. "Mr. Kincaid." He cleared his throat. "Sir, your presence isn't—"

"Stay out of this, Baron."

Caitlin stamped her foot. "How dare you tell him that! Leighton? Why don't you do something?"

"He is," Tyler said, flashing Leighton a chilly smile. "He's minding his own business. Isn't that right, pal?"

"Caitlin," Leighton said, "my dear, perhaps..."

Tyler took Caitlin's elbow, held on to it even as she tried to jerk free.

"McCord," he said softly, "don't drag him into this. This is between you and me."

'It's between you and Jonas," Caitlin said, and waited, oh waited, for him to tell her she was wrong.

He didn't.

Tyler looked at her, then let her go. "You're right," he said gruffly. "It is."

He leaned down, brushed his mouth over hers. Then he walked down the hall toward the library, where her stepfather was waiting. After he'd disappeared around a corner, Leighton came scurrying up beside her.

"Impudent bastard," he muttered.

Caitlin swung around, eyes snapping, but one look at his pale face and sweaty brow stopped her. This was Leighton. What did she expect? Everyone knew what he was. Leighton had to know it, too. Besides, in her heart, she really couldn't blame him for what he'd done—for what he *hadn't* done, when he saw Tyler kiss her. *Oh, be honest, Caitlin!* When he saw her kiss Tyler back.

The scene must have been raw enough to send any onlooker scurrying for cover. Even afterward, when she'd pulled away and Tyler had talked to her, the power emanating from him had been almost palpable. She honestly couldn't imagine any man standing up to him...well, with the exception of her stepbrothers.

They wouldn't have been afraid to take him on. In fact, Gage, Travis and Slade reminded her of Tyler. Hard men, when they had to be. Gentle, when being gentle mattered.

And Tyler could be gentle. His touch could be tender, and his kisses...

His kisses.

Caitlin closed her eyes, swayed a little as she remembered those kisses. If she and Tyler had been alone, he'd have finished what had begun the previous night. And she wanted him to. Yes, oh, yes, she wanted him to. She longed to lie beneath him, to watch that handsome, arrogant face lose its composure as she arched up to meet him, as she wrapped her legs around him, took him deep, deep inside her...

"Catie?"

She blinked. Leighton was staring at her, his face still pale under its year-round tan.

"I should have beaten Kincaid to a pulp," he said. "But I didn't want to subject you to any further distress."

Caitlin sighed. "Of course."

"Are you—are you all right?"

She laughed this time and looped her arm through his. "It was only a kiss, Leighton. I'm fine. Well, not really. I'm starving," she said brightly. "Do you think we're too late for brunch?"

Leighton shot a glance down the hall, as if Tyler might suddenly materialize like an image from a bad dream.

"Uh, yes. Yes, I think we probably are. Perhaps another time..."

"Nonsense. I'm hungry as a horse. If we've missed brunch, I'll settle for the buffet at the Hearthstone Inn. How's that sound?"

"It sounds—it sounds fine." He looked towards the library again. "That is, if you really think—I mean, if you really want—"

Caitlin lost her patience. "Dammit, Leighton, isn't that what I just said?"

His feet dragged only a little as she hurried him out the door and down the steps, but he almost stumbled when she led him past the library windows, toward his car.

Oh, hell, she thought, why was she doing this? The last thing she wanted was to spend the next hour in Leighton's company.

Her spine prickled.

Tyler was watching from the window. She could almost feel his eyes on her, boring a hole between her shoulder blades just as she could still feel the imprint of his kiss on her lips.

Suddenly, it seemed difficult to breathe in the hot summer air.

"Hurry, Leighton," she said gaily, and laced her fingers through his.

Jonas usually sat in the armchair that Marta laughingly called his throne.

He always rolled his eyes when she said it but the truth was that he did like sitting in it. It was a high-backed wing chair made of hand-tanned, buttery soft leather. The Espada crest was burned into the back and arms, bull horns bound with rope and pierced by the ancient Spanish sword he'd found decades ago, when he'd sweated and strained to make this land his.

The chair gave him an advantage, imagined or not. When his sons were growing up, he'd always begun disciplinary meetings seated in it with his hands firmly placed over the crests, and he'd helped anoint more than one politician with a word and a check handed over while he sat in that same chair.

But he wasn't sitting in it now.

He was standing, shoulders and spine as straight as a man who'd seen so many winters could make them. Instinct told him it would be a mistake to sit while Tyler Kincaid stood.

Not even his throne chair would give him the advantage, if this conversation were going where he figured it would. Where he feared it would, not because Kincaid had a case worth hearing but because all the old memories had come swarming back. They'd been haunting his days and nights, ever since he'd laid eyes on the man the week before.

It was early, way too early for bourbon, but Jonas poured himself one anyway, drank down half at one gulp, refilled the glass and then stood, waiting, for Kincaid to come in. The bastard took his time about it. And damned if he didn't head for the window the second he walked into the room.

Jonas cleared his throat.

"You wanted to see me," he said coldly, "I'm here, not out there."

Kincaid didn't respond. He didn't turn around, either. He

just kept looking out that window, his posture every bit as rigid as Jonas's, his arms at his sides.

"Dammit, Kincaid..."

Jonas cocked his head. The windows were open; he could hear voices outside. He craned his neck, saw Caitlin and Leighton. What in tarnation had gotten into the girl today? She was hangin' onto the arm of that spineless nephew of his, lookin' up at him and laughin' her head off.

And Kincaid's hands were knotting into fists, as he listened and watched.

Jonas's eyes narrowed. Did he really think he could have his way with Catie? She was a Baron. Well, she was the next best thing to a Baron, and the world would come to an end before he saw her in the arms of—of—

"Kincaid." Jonas crossed the room and stood behind Tyler. "You got business with me, get to it, otherwise get out of my house and off my land."

Tyler forced himself to turn away from the sight outside and turned, slowly, towards Jonas Baron. The old man looked as imperious as a Roman senator but there was a flicker in his eyes that said he wasn't feeling quite as tough as his words, and his looks, suggested.

"You're good at making that threat, Baron."

"Ain't a threat, it's a promise."

Tyler smiled. What he really wanted was to wrap his hands around the old man's throat, but what good would that do, after all these years? He wanted the answers he'd come for. It was too late for vengeance.

Far too late.

"You're good at pretending you don't know why I'm here, either."

"Business, you said."

"No, Baron, I didn't. I said we're going to talk about something that happened thirty-five years ago." Taking his time, he strolled past Jonas to the cabinet where he remembered the liquor was stored and opened it. "It's too early for me to drink bourbon. Have you something else to wet a man's throat?"

Jonas's mouth turned down as he watched Tyler poke

around inside the cabinet. "Makin' yourself at home, ain't you?"

Tyler looked around and smiled. "Sure," he said lazily. "Heck, you know what they say. 'Better late than never.'"

The men's eyes met, and what Jonas saw made an icy fist close around his gut.

"I ain't much for homilies," he said curtly. "You want somethin' else, try that cabinet just underneath."

The cabinet was a small, well-disguised refrigerator. Tyler reached for a bottle, took his time opening it, lifting it to his lips and taking a long swallow. His throat felt parched, like the desert after an extended dry spell, and there was a cramp in his belly, which was dumb. He wasn't nervous. What was there to be nervous about? He was about to confront his past. Put his demons to rest. Solve the puzzle, whatever in hell you wanted to call it, all thanks to an early-morning phone call from the private investigator.

"I hope you're sitting down, sir," Crane had said, in a tone that conjured up a picture of him wringing his hands with delight. "I have some astounding news."

Tyler took another mouthful of ale.

Astounding was the word for it, all right. And that was the way he was determined to treat it, as news that amazed him, not information that had set his gut churning and prompted another dozen questions that needed answering even more desperately than the original.

He took a deep breath and turned to Jonas.

"I asked you some questions, the last time we spoke."

Jonas shrugged his shoulders. "Mebbe."

"Questions about babies born to women on Espada, thirty-five years ago."

"Did you?" Jonas shrugged again. "My memory ain't what it used to be, Kincaid, but if that's what you say—"

"Don't screw with me, old man."

Tyler's words fell like stones between them. Jonas started to answer, saw the tightly controlled fury in the younger man's eyes, and decided keeping quiet might be a better plan.

"I told you I was especially interested in a child born here on or about July 18, thirty-five years ago.'' Tyler put down the bottle of ale and folded his arms over his chest. ''Does that jog your memory, Baron?''

''What if it does?'' Jonas folded his arms, too. ''Get to the point, Kincaid.''

''We talked about a couple of your men whose wives were pregnant that summer.''

''You talked. I listened. And I told you there wasn't a way in hell I could remember details like who had a bun in the oven and who didn't, that far back.''

''You remembered that your housekeeper had given birth that summer.''

''Yeah, well, that's diff'rent. Carmen's been here so long she's part of the family. I put the boy she birthed that summer through medical school.'' Jonas frowned and looked past Tyler to the grandfather clock in the corner. ''I got things to do and places to go, Kincaid. You got somethin' more to tell me, you'd best tell it.''

Tyler put his hands into the back pockets of his jeans. ''What you didn't remember was that your own wife had a baby that summer, too,'' he said. His voice was very soft; the look in his eyes flat and unforgiving. ''How come you didn't mention that, when I asked you who'd had babies on this ranch, on or about July 18, thirty-five summers ago, Baron? How come you managed to forget that Juanita Baron dropped a litter, too?''

Jonas moved fast, much faster than Tyler would have figured a man his age could move. He shot out a hand, caught Tyler by the shirtfront.

''You watch what you say about my wife,'' he growled.

''Take your hand off me, old man.'' Tyler's eyes flashed. ''Take it off, or so help me, I'll do what I've been thinking about doing ever since early this morning, I'll pick you up by your neck and throw you through that damned window!''

The men glared at each other, eye to eye, toe to toe. At last, Jonas let go of Tyler's shirt and took a step back.

''How come?'' Tyler said, very softly.

''I didn't mention it 'cause it was none of your business.''

"I asked you what you knew about babies born on Espada that summer."

"And I answered you." Jonas walked around Tyler, picked up his glass and drank down the rest of his bourbon. His hand trembled; the realization made his stomach turn with self-disgust. "I don't owe you the details, Kincaid, but since you've asked them, I'll tell you. Yeah, my wife—my first wife—was pregnant back then." He looked at his glass, looked at the bottle of bourbon, picked it up and poured another inch of the liquid. "She died in childbirth."

Tyler nodded. "I know that," he said, and waited to feel something, just as he'd waited when the private detective dropped the news on him earlier, but he felt nothing. "She's buried here, on Espada."

"Yeah. Yeah, she is." Jonas tossed back half his drink, wiped the back of his hand across his mouth and walked to the door. "You happy now?"

"Is that what you think I should be?" Tyler said, with a tight smile. "Happy?"

"Why wouldn't you be? You came here, bullied your way into my library, got me to talk about somethin' still hurts me to remember..."

"What does it hurt you to remember, old man?"

"Why, what I just told you. About losin' my wife." Jonas drew a shuddering breath. "Juanita was—she was special."

He means it, Tyler thought, his eyes narrowing as he stared at the lined face. The old man had done what he'd done, but he'd loved his wife.

For the first time since he'd begun his quest, Tyler wondered if he really wanted to push it any further. The deeper he dug, the more impenetrable things became. Maybe it would be better to leave here thinking he'd found the truth, but not certain of it.

No. Hell, no. Tyler straightened his shoulders. He'd never backed away from anything in his life, and he wasn't going to start now.

"Special," he said softly.

Jonas nodded. "That's right."

"So special that you plucked her baby from her womb and gave it away?"

There it was, Jonas thought, the ugly secret was out, dragged from the darkness where he'd thought he'd buried it so many years ago and thrust into a merciless present. He was ready, though. He'd been ready ever since the day Tyler Kincaid had confronted him. Truth was, he'd been half expecting this moment for a long time.

Thirty-five years ago, he'd still been young enough to believe a man with power and money could dig a hole so deep the secret he dropped into it would never be found. But a lot had happened since then. Governments had fallen. Presidents had tumbled. No secret was safe, really safe, anymore...not unless you were the only one who kept it.

Jonas sighed. "Kincaid," he said, "you amaze me."

"The feeling's mutual. You amaze me, too, Baron. I once beat the crap out of a man I caught trying to dump a puppy in the river." Tyler's voice roughened and he took a step forward. "Just imagine what I want to do to you."

"You amaze me, boy, because you've got one hell of an imagination. 'Plucked the child from her womb and gave it away?' Is that what you're accusin' me of?"

"Yes," Tyler said coldly. "That's exactly what I'm accusing you of."

"Well, I hate to derail this train from wherever you're tryin' to take it, Kincaid, but the simple fact of the matter is, my Juanita died and her baby died with her."

"Her baby?"

"*Our* baby," Jonas said, mentally cursing himself for the slip. "It was the tragedy of my life, Kincaid, losin' my beloved wife and my child in the blink of an eye."

"A tremendous tragedy. So huge that you married again, a year later."

"Well, what can I tell you, boy? I'm a man who needs a woman at his—"

Jonas gasped as Tyler's hand shot out and curled into the collar of his shirt.

"You lying old bastard," he snarled, as he hoisted Jonas to

his toes. "That child didn't die. You got rid of it. You threw your son away, as if he were garbage."

"It ain't true," Jonas croaked. "He's dead, I tell you. He died before he could take his first—"

"Liar! No good, goddamned liar!" Tyler flung the old man from him. God, he was so close to the edge. So close. It had felt good, having his hand around that wattled neck.

"You get out," Jonas said. "Get out now, Kincaid, before I have your sorry ass hauled off my ranch."

"Stop bluffing, Baron. I know the truth, and all the denials in the world won't change it. You must have paid the doctor who attended the delivery a small fortune. Or maybe you had something hanging over his head. Whatever it was, it was enough to get him to sign the death certificate but not enough to keep him from hating himself, from drowning the memory of what he'd done in a bottle—and from telling someone about it, someone who's willing to go into court and testify."

"Who?" Jonas demanded, and then he bit his lip. "Not that it matters. I don't know what you're talkin' about."

"And then there's the grave, up on the hill." Tyler puffed out a breath. "The one that's supposed to hold my—to hold your first wife, and her dead baby." He watched Jonas's face drain of color. "Yes," he said quietly, "that's right, old man. Think about that grave, and what's really in it, and what would happen if it were dug up."

Jonas seemed to shrink inside his skin. He reached out a hand, felt for his armchair and sank into it.

"All right." His voice was flat. "The only body in that there grave is Juanita's. Is that what you wanted to hear?"

Was it? Tyler swallowed dryly. Now that the moment had arrived, he wasn't so sure. He'd been positive he knew what he wanted. Answers. The puzzle solved. The mystery of who he was, and why he'd been abandoned at birth, unraveled.

But the phone call from the investigator had changed everything.

"Kincaid?"

Tyler jerked his head up. Jonas Baron was looking at him with all the hatred in the world shining in his eyes.

"Do yourself a favor, boy. Don't ask no more questions. Jes' turn around, walk out that door, and the both of us'll forget you were ever here. Okay?"

"No," Tyler answered, even though it was hard not to do just that. "No, it's not okay. I need one last answer."

Jonas grinned mirthlessly. "Thought you might. All right, ask it, then."

Tyler took a deep breath. His heart, his blood, the entire world seemed to stand still.

"I want to know," he said quietly, "why you gave me away."

CHAPTER NINE

TYLER regretted the question as soon as he'd asked it.

He'd come to demand the truth, not to plead for it. And, he thought angrily, that was how he'd sounded, as if he were begging for an explanation.

Hell. What did it matter, how the question sounded? He'd found what he'd come for and more, something he'd never imagined—something he couldn't comprehend.

He'd thought of all of the plausible reasons to explain why he'd been given up at birth. He could almost see his mother as a young girl, frightened and alone, so desperate she'd seen no way out but to get rid of her baby. Even so, he'd never been able to figure out how she could have dumped him on a doorstep and never looked back.

Now he had the explanation, and it drove the knife deeper into his heart. His mother hadn't been a desperate kid, she'd been a woman. She'd died, giving him life, and her husband— the man who'd sired him—had tossed him out as if he were trash.

Pain shot through him again and he shoved it aside and filled the yawning chasm it left with rage.

"Answer me, you son of a bitch," he growled, and swung toward Jonas. "Why did you do it? How could you take your own flesh and blood and throw it away?"

"You weren't thrown away," Jonas said coldly. "I made all the necessary arrangements for your disposal."

"For my disposal," Tyler said, very softly. A muscle knotted in his jaw.

"I ain't gonna play word games, Kincaid. You asked for the truth. Well, that's what I'm tellin' you, and if it ain't pretty enough to suit you, that's just too damned bad."

Tyler balled his hands into fists and shoved them deep into his pockets. "Go on."

Jonas walked to the sideboard, took the bottle of bourbon and poured another couple of inches of it into his glass.

"It wasn't all that difficult. I had me a contact in Atlanta, a lawyer I'd done business with." He tilted the glass to his lips and drank. "He wasn't the sort the Chamber of Commerce likes to talk about but he knew how to handle my problem. He came up with a story to tell you, once you was old enough, 'bout being found on a doorstep somewhere. Got you a birth certificate and put a name on it—"

"John Smith," Tyler said softly, his eyes locked on the old man's face.

Jonas shrugged. "Maybe. It's been a long time. Anyways, the lawyer did everything that needed doin'. Worked up a good story, made you legal, gave you to people who agreed to raise you, right and proper." Jonas drank some more of the bourbon. "Wrote a fat check, to make sure they would."

"Not fat enough," Tyler said coldly. "It must have run out, by the time they died."

"So I heard. I done some checkin' of my own, since you turned up." Jonas took a cigar from his shirt pocket, bit off the tip and spat it into an ashtray. "Anyways, you done all right for yourself, far as I can see."

"Oh, yes," Tyler said, with another terrible smile, "I've done all right for myself."

"Well, then." Jonas put down the glass and wiped the back of his hand across his mouth. "You came for answers, you got 'em. Far as I can see, that finishes our business." He walked to the door and opened it. "It's Sunday, boy. My one and only day of rest. I'd appreciate it if—'

Tyler slammed the door and stood in front of it, his arms folded over his chest.

"Why?"

"Why, what?"

"Don't play games with me, you old son of a bitch!" He could feel the adrenaline pumping through his body, feel his hands trembling again with the need to put them around

Jonas's neck. "You tell me why you gave away your own flesh and blood."

"That's just the point, boy." Jonas's voice was hard and cold. "You weren't my flesh and blood. My wife had been unfaithful. Took herself a lover, some no-good drifter come through here with slick looks and a fancy way with words." His mouth twisted. "You were his whelp, not mine."

"My moth... Your wife told you that?"

The old man laughed. "Hell, no. She put horns on me, but she wasn't stupid. Juanita insisted you were mine, right to the second she went into labor. Figured if she could talk hard enough, fast enough, I'd believe her." Jonas's eyes narrowed to slits. "But I could count, Kincaid. She'd turned me out of her bed nine months before. The only man could have been in that bed was the drifter."

Tyler jammed his hands into his pockets and walked across the room. It was too much to absorb, too much to accept. His mother had died giving him life, his father wasn't this old man but a drifter...

"Who was he?" He swung around, stared at Jonas. "My father. What was his name?"

"I don't remember. Hell, it don't matter a damn anyways. I heard he got hisself killed, tryin' to jump a freight train couple a months after I ran him off. You got any more questions?"

Tyler shook his head. He already had more answers than he could handle. He was the unwanted by-product of an illicit liaison between an unfaithful woman and a drifter. Knowing the story, he couldn't even blame Jonas Baron for his actions. Sure, he could have handled things differently. He could have put the baby up for adoption through regular channels and sure, maybe his life—Tyler's life—would have been easier...

But life was what you made of it, and he'd done the best he could, with his.

The old man's rage was understandable. What man could survive the knowledge that his woman had lain in another man's arms? If Caitlin ever gave herself to someone else, if she ever hungered for another man's kisses...

"I asked you somethin', Kincaid. You got any more questions, or are we finished?"

"We're finished," Tyler said, and cleared his throat.

Jonas nodded. "That we are. And if you got any damned fool ideas about Espada, you better forget them."

"Espada?" Tyler repeated. "What ideas would I have about Espada?"

"Come on, boy. I'm old but I ain't senile. There's talk everywhere about this ranch, and how I ain't got a son to leave it to."

"I hate to disillusion you, Baron, but hard as this may be to grasp, nobody talks about Espada where I come from. And unless I've misunderstood every mention your stepdaughter's made of her brothers, you have three sons to leave it to."

"Not a one of 'em wants it."

Tyler nodded. "Yeah, well, that's very interesting, but—"

"Maybe you figure to have some claim on it." Jonas eyed him narrowly. "Maybe you already knew all that stuff I just told you, about my Juanita. Maybe that's why you really come here, 'cause you thought you could make a case that Espada ought to be yours."

"What?"

"You heard me, boy. You lied your way onto my land and now, for all I know, you're gonna lie and say I'm the man who fathered you."

Tyler grabbed Jonas by the shirt. "You call me 'boy' and accuse me of lying again and I'll—I'll—" He looked at his hand, knotted into Jonas's shirt, made a sound of disgust and let go. "Listen to me, Baron, and listen good. I came here for one reason, and it didn't have a damned thing to do with your ranch. Why in hell would I want it? It's nothing to me, just acres of dirt and cows."

"Them acres of dirt and cows is worth millions."

"You did some checking of your own, you said. Then you know I don't need your money."

"Money ain't everything."

Tyler smiled thinly. "Is that advice? Or is it wisdom gleaned from your advanced years?"

"It's fact, Kincaid. Ain't a man alive don't want his birthright."

"His birthright," Tyler said, lifting an eyebrow.

"There are some might say I denied you that. You would have had my name, if I hadn't caught your mama with the drifter." Jonas tossed aside the unlit cigar. "Bet you hate me for that."

A muscle flexed in Tyler's jaw. "I don't hate you. You did what you had to do, that's all."

"Come on, Kincaid, be honest. On account of me, you ended up livin' with people who got paid to take you in. And when they was gone, you went into a state home."

"There are worse things," Tyler said coldly.

"There surely are." Jonas smiled slyly. "Things like that there ranch where the court put you, after you got yourself in trouble."

"If there's a point to all this," Tyler said, even more coldly, "get to it."

"Oh, there's a point, all right. Seems to me is that it had to be a mighty temptin' idea, you comin' here to claim you was a Baron."

"You just finished telling me I'm not." Tyler smiled thinly. "And the better I know you, old man, the happier that makes me."

"My firstborn came along three years after you."

"The lucky bastard," Tyler said, and grinned mirthlessly.

"And I'll tell you right now, I ain't takin' no fancy tests to prove you ain't of my blood."

"Are you crazy? Did I even suggest you take tests to prove it?"

"I'm jes' tellin' you, loud and clear, you get yourself some fancy lawyer to talk about genes and chro-mo-somes and such, I'll turn my lawyers on you an' him both, and grind you into dog meat." Jonas jabbed a finger into Tyler's chest. "You got that?"

Tyler caught Jonas's arm. The muscles were ropy and as hard as steel cables, but Tyler was stronger and more power-

ful. He twisted the arm behind Jonas's back until the older
man grunted with the pain.

"You son of a bitch," Tyler said softly. "You're not sure
you *aren't* the man who fathered me."

"That's bull patties."

"You threw out a baby like it was garbage and all the time
you knew that child might have been yours."

"No way. You couldn't have been mine. I told you, Juanita
locked me out of her room for the better part of a long, cold
year…except for—"

"Except?"

Jonas jerked his arm free. "Except for the one time I broke
down that door and took what was mine to take, despite the
fact that you was probably already in the oven."

"You don't know that."

"You ain't mine, Kincaid. I know that, and nothing my wife
said then or you say now will change it." He strode to the
door and yanked it open. "You came for the truth and I gave
it to you. It isn't my fault you can't deal with it."

Tyler put his hands into his pockets and rocked back on his
heels.

"My oh my," he said softly. "Wouldn't that make for the
start of one hell of an obituary? 'Jonas Baron, patriarch of the
Baron clan. He carved out a kingdom and gave away his firstborn son.'" He smiled slyly. "Damn, but it's almost biblical."

"Get out!"

"Did she know? My mother. Did she know you gave me
away?"

"I told you, she died." He shot Tyler a hate-filled look.
"But she damned well knew I wasn't gonna be fool enough
to raise a child that wasn't my own. I told her that when I
first saw you was growin' in her belly."

Tyler nodded. He imagined a woman with features like his,
carrying him beneath her heart, imagined the pain she must
have felt, hearing her husband say he wanted no part of her
child…

Imagined her breathing her last, even as she struggled to
give him life.

He pictured his mother as he'd never been able to see her before. She had a Spanish name. That might explain the midnight-blackness of his hair, the high cheekbones. She was taking on shape and substance for him now; she was a human being, a desperate woman trapped in a marriage to a man she must have hated, forced to endure the agony of wondering what would happen to her child, when it was born.

Tyler saw all this, and it broke his heart.

His breathing quickened. His muscles tightened. He wanted to beat Jonas Baron to the ground, stand over him as he struggled to get up and hit him and hit him until he went down and couldn't get up.

The boy he'd once been would have done it. But he was a man now. He lived by a moral code. Despite his start in life, he'd grown up to be someone the woman who'd borne him would have been proud to acknowledge as her son.

Knowing that, believing it, was all that kept his hands knotted but at his sides.

"Are you deaf, Kincaid? I want you out of here."

It was hard, gathering himself together, but Tyler did.

"I know what you want, Baron." He walked to the door, pausing when he reached it, his eyes locked to Jonas's. "You want life in your little kingdom to go on, the same as it always has. You want to crack the whip and watch your subjects jump." Tyler's smile glittered, glittered even more brightly when he saw the flash of apprehension in Jonas's eyes. "Well, those days are coming to an end," he said, almost gently. "You know those blood tests you mentioned? The ones to do with genes and chromosomes?" Tyler reached out, smoothed down Jonas's shirtfront. "You're going to take them. A whole battery of them." His smile tilted. "And when they're done, and I've proved that you and I are father and son—"

"You'll never prove that!"

"I will," Tyler said, and meant it. He knew his mother now; knew, deep inside his soul, that she wouldn't have violated her marriage vows, even if she'd made them with a man like Jonas Baron. "And after I have, the next thing I'm going to do is claim my birthright—isn't that what you called it? Claim it, as your eldest son, and do it while you're still alive, so that I can tell you, every day of your life right up to the minute you breathe your last, that once Espada is mine I'm going to cut it into little pieces and sell every last one of them, until nothing remains of you or this place, not even a memory.''

Jonas's face went white. ''I'll fight you.''

''Fight me.'' Tyler smiled. ''That'll make the victory all the sweeter.''

''Bastard,'' Jonas said.

Tyler laughed, walked out of the library and out of the house, with Jonas's curses ringing after him.

Day gave way to dusk, and dusk to night.

Tyler stood on the deck of his house in the rolling hills outside Austin. It was dark; the moon had yet to rise and the clouds were playing hide-and-seek with the stars.

He stood with one hip leaning against the wooden railing and a chilled bottle of ale in his hand. He'd been drinking everything from scotch to rye all day and he was still stone-cold sober. The liquor hadn't even washed the bitter taste from his mouth.

He doubted anything could.

He sighed, rolled the cold bottle across his aching forehead and told himself that he was a stupid SOB.

''It's the truth, Kincaid,'' he said aloud. ''You are one really stupid son of a bitch.''

What was he doing in Texas? He had a home, he had a life, back in Georgia. The home was handsome and the life was one he'd enjoyed, until he'd let a meddling mistress and a surprise birthday party turn his existence upside down.

No. No, that wasn't true. Adrianna wasn't to blame, and only a fool would try to lay this off on a party. He'd done it all to himself. He was the one who'd left everything behind and set off on this insane search for his roots.

For his birthright.

Tyler's mouth twisted. He could still hear Jonas's voice inside his head, saying the word with contempt.

He sighed, tilted the bottle to his mouth and drank.

The old man was nuts. Why would he need a birthright? He lived in a world of his own making. Tyler Kincaid's private kingdom, every bit as large and valuable as Espada. Besides, this wasn't about Espada. It was about the mother he'd never known. The hurt she must have felt, each time Jonas made a point of reminding her that he had no intention of acknowledging her child, or of raising it.

And yes, it was about that child, as well. About the boy who'd grown up without a kind touch or a soft word. Without a name. A boy who'd had to fight for the respect he'd been able to force from other boys just like him.

Tyler put down the empty bottle, clasped the railing with both hands and closed his eyes.

The intelligent thing would be to clear out. He couldn't change what had happened, to his mother or to himself. What he ought to do was pack his things, get into his car and drive straight out of Texas. Drive until he reached Atlanta and the life he'd created there. Until he reached his home, the corporation that carried his name…

And Adrianna.

She'd left another message on his machine, her tone perky and upbeat, as if they'd never quarreled. There was a new gallery opening, she'd said, and had he received his invitation to the Forsythe's dinner party next week? Perhaps they could go together, if he was free, if he could possibly make it.

The real message had rung through as clear as a bell, despite all the chatter. Adrianna wanted him back, and on his terms. No ties. No strings. No explanations of why he'd broken off their relationship or where he'd gone.

Tyler opened his eyes and looked blindly into the night.

It was tempting. She was beautiful. She came from his world—from the world he'd made his, anyway. She fit into his life perfectly, without making a ripple.

But she wasn't Caitlin.

Adrianna smelled of expensive perfume, not flowers. Tyler smiled. Not of horse, either, and certainly never of honest sweat as Caitlin sometimes did. Adrianna's hair was always perfect, as if she'd just come from the salon. Caitlin's gener-

ally looked as if she'd brushed the silky mass free of tangles
and then given up.

Adrianna was elegant. Caitlin was...she was exciting.
Everything about her stirred him. Her scent. Her mouth, with
its slightly full lower lip. Her body, so boyish-looking within
her rough and ready jeans and T-shirts and yet so feminine
and rich, when he'd sought her flesh beneath the clothes.

When she'd gone into his arms, last night.

He knew the taste of her mouth, but what would the rest of
her taste like? Honey, he thought. Or sweet cream. Her breasts
would fill his mouth, assuage the endless hunger that had been
in his belly since the first time he'd seen her.

Tyler laughed softly and drank the rest of the ale.

He was turning himself on, just standing here and thinking
about Caitlin McCord. *Turning* himself on? Hell, why lie
about it? He was turned on already, hard as a rock and aching
with need for a woman he hardly knew...

For a woman he couldn't have. She was a Baron, or the
next best thing to it. She was Jonas's stepdaughter and if it
was the last thing he did, he was going to make the old man
choke on his lies.

He was going to destroy him, and you didn't bed a man's
stepdaughter before you slipped a knife between his ribs, even
if you were doing it figuratively.

"Tyler?"

The voice was soft and familiar. Tyler told himself it was
an hallucination, that the alcohol had worked. But when he
turned she was really there, standing in the doorway, the soft
glow from the living room just behind her defining her face
in a play of light and shadow.

"Tyler," she said again, but he didn't answer. He just stood
drinking in the sight of her. She was wearing high-heeled sandals and a dress like the one she'd worn last night. Her hair
hung loose over her shoulders. She looked fragile and feminine and incredibly beautiful, and even though he knew it was
wrong, he hated her for coming here and for reminding him
of how badly he wanted her.

And for reminding him that he could never have her.

"What are you doing here?" he said gruffly.

"I—I..." He saw the long column of her throat move as she swallowed. "I came to say goodbye."

He smiled, and he knew from the way her eyes widened that his smile had not been pleasant.

"Goodbye?" he said lazily. "Are you going away?"

"No. I mean, of course not."

She wore a narrow gold chain around her throat. She touched her fingers to it. It was a nervous gesture and seeing it made him feel good. She was apprehensive and she damned well should be. She had no right, coming here, making him remember how it felt to kiss her, to touch her.

"Jonas said...he said you were leaving."

He walked toward her slowly, his eyes on hers. He could see the race of her pulse in the hollow of her throat. Don't touch her, his mind shouted, dammit, man, don't touch her...and he didn't. He only bent his head and put his mouth against her throat.

"I didn't..." He heard her catch her breath, felt the tremor race through her. "Tyler, please. I didn't come here for—I didn't come here for that."

"Yes," he said softly. "Yes, you did."

He took her face in his hands and lifted it to his. Eyes open, still locked on hers, he kissed her.

It was like touching a match to dry kindling. She moaned, grasped his wrists with her hands, fought for control and found it.

"I told you why I came. Jonas said—"

"To hell with Jonas," he said, and as he did, he knew it was true. His hatred for Jonas had nothing to do with this. With Caitlin.

With what they needed from each other.

He kissed her more hungrily, his mouth moving against hers, the tip of his tongue touching the seam of her lips. She moaned again, touched her hands to his chest, and he forgot everything but her.

"Cait," he said urgently, "my Cait."

Tyler gathered her into his arms, brought her against his

body, heard her little whisper of surprise when she felt his hardness. She flattened her palms against his chest and pulled back.

"Don't. Tyler, don't."

"Say it as if you mean it, and I'll stop."

He nuzzled the hair back from her face, bit gently on her earlobe. He felt her heartbeat leap against his.

"I—I can't stay. I'm having dinner with Leighton."

"You had lunch with Leighton," he said, and kissed her neck.

"I didn't. I couldn't. I—I didn't want to. I was—I was just using him because I was angry at you."

Tyler smiled against her throat. "I know."

"And—and I felt awful about it. So I figured I'd stop by and ask him if he'd like to have dinner…"

Tyler slipped one strap off her shoulder and pressed his mouth to her skin. She caught her breath. Her hands knotted into his shirt.

"You're trying to seduce me," she whispered.

His laughter was low and rough. "And am I succeeding?"

"No," she said, clutching him harder while she rose on her toes and met his questing mouth with her own.

"Open to me," he whispered, and with a groan, she did, parting her lips to his tongue, lifting her hands, tangling them in his hair and pulling his head down to hers.

Tyler shuddered. He bunched her skirt in his hands, lifted it, stroked the softness of her thighs, then cupped her heat, glorying in the sweet dampness that would soon welcome him home.

"Tell me why you came here," he said hoarsely. "Dammit, tell me."

Caitlin drew back and looked into his eyes.

"For this." Her voice broke. "For this. For—"

Tyler crushed her mouth beneath his as he swung her into his arms.

She clung to him as he carried her through the dark house, to his bedroom, to his bed. He lowered her the length of his body, doing it slowly, feeling her softness against his hardness, feeding on her little sighs and whispers as he undressed her.

"Tyler. You should know... I have to tell you..."

"Hush," he said softly, and stopped her words with a kiss. Whatever she wanted to tell him could wait. He needed her, now. Wanted her, now. He had to possess her, before he exploded.

He'd thought about this first time with her, knew it would be fast, but now that she was in his arms he warned himself not to let it happen that way.

Be tender, he told himself. Go slowly. Instinct warned him she hadn't been with many men, and he had to make this right. He wanted to pleasure her until she came apart in his arms, wanted to watch her face as it happened, wanted to do all that before he entered her.

But he was shaking, burning with the need to possess her. Another minute, he'd be incapable of anything but ripping off her panties, unzipping his fly and burying himself deep inside her.

He kissed her again, left her only long enough to switch on a lamp and fight for control. When he turned to her again and stripped off his shirt, he saw a delicate flush rise in her cheeks.

"You're beautiful," she whispered, and she touched him, running her hand lightly over his chest, stroking the tapering line of dark hair that arrowed down his belly. She hesitated, looked up and into his eyes, and cupped her hand over the straining denim that defined the power of what she'd done to him.

He groaned, covered her hand with his, endured that sweet, yearning touch as long as he could without going crazy.

"You're the one who's beautiful," he said, and he drew her close and undid the long zipper down the back of her dress.

Her eyes turned to a smoky gold. She watched his face as he undressed her. He did it slowly, as slowly as he could manage without coming apart. She trembled under the brush of his hands, sighed as he bared her to his eyes and mouth, and when she stood before him, wearing only a wisp of white lace and her high-heeled sandals, he knelt before her, curved his hands around her hips, kissed his way down her belly.

She trembled.

"Oh," she whispered, "oh, Lord…"

He pulled the wisp of lace aside, touched her. Felt the dew of her feminine heart against his hand, and then he put his mouth to her, stroked her with his tongue, kissed her and caressed her until she cried out. He rose then, scooped her into his arms, and brought her down onto the bed.

"Tyler," she said, in a voice filled with wonder. "Tyler…"

She held her arms up to him and he went into them, kissing her mouth, her throat, kissing her breasts, exulting in the taste of her honey-sweet skin. She moaned and arched toward him as he kissed her mouth again and stroked his tongue against hers.

"Please," she sobbed, "Tyler, please…"

"You belong to me," he said fiercely, as he parted her thighs.

"Yes," she said, "yes, oh, yes, Tyler, yes…"

He kissed her again and she returned his kisses the same way, with hunger, not with tenderness, her need for him as complete as her surrender. She tugged at his jeans, making desperate little cries, and he rolled away from her, yanked down his zipper, kicked off his boots, his jeans, his shorts, and she lifted her arms to him, her eyes as deep and dark as the night.

"Come into me," she whispered. "Tyler, please, take me. Take me…"

And, on one long, possessive, silken thrust, he did.

CHAPTER TEN

HAD hours gone by, or was it only moments?

Caitlin couldn't tell. She'd shattered in Tyler's arms, shattered into a million pieces and soared with him into the hot, molten heart of the sun. Now, lying beneath him, her heart still racing against his, his face buried in her throat, she knew that nothing in her life had prepared her for tonight.

Giving herself to Tyler had changed her, forever.

She sighed, stirred in his embrace.

He felt her shift beneath him. "I'm crushing you," he said softly, but when he tried to roll off her, she shook her head and tightened her arms around him.

"Stay," she whispered, and closed her eyes, not trusting herself to say more because her throat felt constricted, as if she might weep, and she didn't want that to happen.

If she wept, how would she explain that it was from joy and not from sorrow?

"Stay with me," she whispered again, and she felt his lips curve against her throat.

He was holding her close. And it felt so right to lie with him this way, with his body over hers, protecting her. She could feel the beat of his heart as it steadied and slowed, smell his scent. The taste of him lingered on her mouth.

He was still inside her, still a part of her, joined to her in a way she'd never been joined with any man before.

And she was glad, so glad, that Tyler had been the first.

She hadn't planned it this way; she'd never consciously thought about "saving" herself for any one man. There'd been opportunities. Boys in high school, even one she'd gone steady with. There'd been boys during the two years she'd spent away at college, too, and once in a while she went to the movies or

138

out dancing with a nice guy who was the foreman of a neighboring ranch.

The thing of it was, there'd never been anyone who really mattered.

Sometimes, she'd even wondered if she was lacking something. She had a secret passion for romance novels and for movies that made her cry. She kept those things to herself because it was tough enough riding herd on a bunch of cowboys and standing up to Jonas without having anybody know about her secret vices. She'd decided that maybe she was just one of those women who found their passion in make-believe worlds, not in the real one.

That was okay. It was safer.

And yet—and yet, what she'd felt in Tyler's arms put her "secret passions" into perspective. Fantasy didn't stand up to reality. His touch, his kisses, the way he'd made love to her...

Nothing, *nothing,* had prepared for this night.

Tyler whispered her name, rose on one elbow and kissed her mouth. He took his time doing it, sucking on her bottom lip, teasing her lips open, stroking the tip of his tongue against hers. Sensation after sensation raced through her, turning her inside out, threatening to stop her heart.

It was just a kiss, and it thrilled her.

"You taste delicious," he said softly.

Caitlin smiled. "So do you."

"Like..." He frowned, bent to her, kissed her again. "I can't decide. Like whipped cream? Honey?" Gently he nibbled her mouth. "Or maybe cotton candy."

"Cotton candy?" she said, and laughed.

"Mmm. Pink cotton candy, and I've always had a weakness for pink cotton candy." He smiled, stroked her hair back from her face. "Cait? Are you all right?"

She nodded. "Yes."

"Sweetheart, you should have told me."

Caitlin blushed. "I tried to."

Suddenly she felt unaccountably shy. It was silly, considering what they had just done, but there was something about lying naked in a man's arms and discussing the loss of your virginity...

"Yeah." His voice was rough. "I was beyond listening."

"Would it—would it have mattered?"

Tyler caught an auburn curl in his fingers and brought it to his mouth. "I'd have gone slower," he said softly, "or I'd have tried to. Did I hurt you?"

"No. Oh, no. You didn't hurt me. It was—it was—"

"Wonderful," he said gently.

"Yes. Incredible. I thought my heart would—would—"

"Burst? Yes, I know." He rolled to his side and took her with him, still holding her, still inside her, still wondering how such a miracle could have happened. He was a man who believed in equality. He'd never condemned a woman in his life for having the same sexual appetites and experience a man had, but that moment when he'd felt that fragile barrier, when he'd realized he was Caitlin's first lover... He gave her a lingering, tender kiss. "That's how it was for me, too."

"I'm glad." She felt the rush of heat in her face and knew she was blushing. "I mean, some men might not be thrilled to find themselves making love to—to—"

Tyler slipped his hand into Caitlin's hair, watched as the colors of autumn slid through his fingers.

"A virgin," he said softly.

"Yes. Oh, it's such an old-fashioned word."

"It's a beautiful word," Tyler whispered, and kissed her again.

Caitlin sighed and snuggled closer in his arms. "I'm glad you think so."

"What man wouldn't?"

"Well, you have to remember..." She smiled and touched her hand to his face. "I grew up with three brothers."

"Stepbrothers," he said quickly. "You're not really related to Jonas."

"Of course not." Her smile tilted. "He never lets me forget that."

"Hell," Tyler said, and leaned his forehead against hers. "I didn't mean... I just..." *Tell her,* a voice inside suddenly said, *tell her why you needed to say that, that you had to remind her that there's no Baron blood in her veins. Tell her the truth. Who you think you are. Hell, who you know you are. That you're a Baron, but your own father got rid of you...*

"Tyler?"

He blinked and focused on Caitlin's face. Her eyes were dark with concern. Concern, for him. No one, no woman, had ever looked at him that way.

"Tyler, what is it?" She lifted her hand to his cheek and he turned his face, pressed his mouth against her palm. "I know you and Jonas dislike each other, but he's been good to me. He raised me. And now—"

Tyler silenced her with a kiss. These moments belonged to the two of them. The last thing he wanted was to hear the woman in his arms defend the son of a bitch he was going to destroy. And he had to destroy him. It was either that or spend the rest of his life consumed by hatred.

"So," he said, with deliberate lightness, "what were you going to tell me about your stepbrothers? Don't tell me they were the ones who sat you down and told you about the birds and the bees."

Caitlin laughed. "Are you kidding? Nobody told me about birds and bees, Tyler. I learned about stallions and mares the day I wandered into our stables when one of our studs—"

Our stables. Our studs. She wasn't a Baron, the old man wouldn't let her forget that she wasn't, but that was the way she thought of herself, as a Baron, as someone who loved Espada almost as much as he despised it.

"—Slade, I think it was, turned around and saw me. I thought he was going to pass out. My stepbrothers, tell me about sex? They taught me to rope horses and herd cows, but sex was for other girls, not for their little sister." She grinned. "They waited up for me, after my first date."

"They did, huh?"

"They loved me," she said simply, "and I loved them. Of course..." She laughed softly and traced the outline of Tyler's lips with the tip of her finger. "Of course, that didn't keep me from trying to beat them up. Well, one at a time, naturally."

"Naturally." Tyler grinned and rolled her beneath him. "I'm impressed."

"See, they had this club..."

"Mmm." He bent his head, nuzzled her hair from her throat. "Los Lobos."

"Yes." She bit back a moan as he brushed his mouth against the skin at the delicate juncture of neck and shoulder. "That's right. I told you about—about—"

Tyler caught her hands and held them. "Go on," he said softly, as he kissed the hollow of her throat, the slope of her breast. She could feel his lips curve into a smile against her flesh. "Don't let me distract you."

Caitlin closed her eyes. "It was—it was just the three of them," she said, in a breathless flurry of softly whispered words. "And eventually they made me a member, but when they got older, they sometimes met without me in the hayloft...oh. Oh, Tyler..."

"They met in the hayloft," he said, as he cupped her breasts and rubbed his thumbs across the yearning tips. "Without you."

"Without me. I guess they talked about—" Her voice broke. He was kissing her belly, her thighs, biting gently at the soft, tender flesh. "About girls," she said, in a choked whisper. "And—and one time, I heard them talking about virgins and agreeing that—that..." Caitlin's hips arched from the bed. "I can't think when—when..." She cried out and he moved up her body and kissed her mouth, drinking in her cries, glorying in her surrender.

"They were boys, sweetheart," he whispered, slipping his hands under her bottom. "And maybe they knew that taking a girl's virginity is a hell of a responsibility."

"Yes." She made a soft little sound as he parted her thighs. "That's why I thought you might not be pleased when you realized—when you realized—"

He entered her slowly this time, holding back, sliding into her easily, spinning out the ecstasy of the moment, watching her eyes fill with his image as her body filled with his heat, watching as the pleasure caught her up in a surging wave of desire.

"You gave me a gift." He moved, then moved again. She rose to him, sobbed out his name as she put her arms around him, as she closed around him like a satin sheath. "An incredible gift. Cait," he said thickly, "Cait..."

Cait, my love, he thought.

And then he stopped thinking and spilled himself deep inside her again.

When the first light of the new day touched the hills, Caitlin sat up and looked out the window.

"Look," she said. "Tyler, what a glorious sight."

Tyler leaned on his elbow and propped his head on his hand. "Glorious," he agreed lazily, and stroked his fingers lightly over her breasts. Despite the long night they'd shared, his caress brought a telling flush of desire to her face.

The sight, the knowledge that just his touch could arouse her, filled him with possessive pleasure.

"I'm talking about the sunrise," she said, with a little laugh.

"Mmm." Tyler ran his hand up Caitlin's throat, gently cupped her face and brought her mouth to his for a kiss. "Want to go outside and watch it?"

"Oh, yes. Just give me a minute to get dr... Tyler?" She squealed as he rose from the bed and lifted her, and the blanket she clutched, into his arms. "Tyler," she said, as he strode toward the patio doors, "we can't..."

Her protests were useless. Tyler opened the sliding doors, stepped out into the awakening morning, wrapped them both within the king-size blanket and sat down in one of the patio chairs with her in his lap.

'We can do anything we want," he said smugly, "because we're the only two people on the planet."

Caitlin's smile faded. If only it were true. If only she and Tyler were alone...but they weren't. Jonas stood between them like an omnipresent apparition. What venom there'd been in his voice, when he'd spoken Tyler's name last night.

"He's up to no good, missy. You'll see."

"You're wrong," she'd said, and Jonas had looked at her and smiled slyly, the way he always did just before he raked in the chips.

She shivered.

"Sweetheart?" Tyler's arms tightened around her. "Are you cold? Shall we go inside?"

"No. Oh, no. I just—I just felt a chill for a second, that's all."

He drew her closer and gently urged her head onto his shoulder. Her body was soft and warm; her hair was a tangled skein of silk against his cheek. She smelled sweetly mysterious, her perfume a subtle blending of memories of the passion-filled night and the promise of the new day, and he wasn't sure which he wanted more, to just go on sitting with her in his arms, holding her close and inhaling her fragrance, or to spread the blanket in the grass and make love to her again.

"Comfortable?" he whispered, pressing a kiss to her temple.

Caitlin sighed. "Mmm."

"You're sure you're warm enough?"

"Mmm."

Tyler chuckled, leaned back in the chair and rested his chin on the top of her head.

"I like a woman who's easy to please," he said softly.

She sighed, turned her face toward him and kissed his throat. "Jonas wouldn't agree," she said, before she could stop herself.

"That old bastard." His voice hardened, but she knew, from the way his arms tightened around her, that the sudden edge she heard had nothing to do with her. "How in hell do you put up with him?"

"He's a difficult man, I agree. But—"

"Oh, hell." Tyler caught her chin in his hand, lifted her face to his and kissed her. "The last thing I want to do is argue over Jonas Baron." He smiled, kissed her again, lingering over the sweetness of her mouth. "Tell me about Caitlin McCord."

Caitlin smiled back. "You want the one-minute story, or the two?"

"I want to know everything about her." He stroked a fingertip along her lips. "What kind of little girl was she?"

"A tomboy," she said instantly. "A skinny kid with knobby knees and sharp elbows." She laughed softly. "That's what Gage always said, anyway."

"Gage." Tyler forced himself to smile. "One of the Barons."

"The youngest, yes. You'd like him."

"I doubt it." Tyler's smile glittered. "Not if he's anything like his old man."

"Oh, he isn't. None of my stepbrothers are anything like their father."

"Well, that takes the whole lot of them up a notch in my estimation, sight unseen."

"They've all made their own ways in the world."

Tyler's brows lifted. "Baron didn't set them up in whatever it is they do?"

Caitlin laughed. "Set them up? No way. They defied him, Tyler. Each and every one of them." Sighing, she snuggled closer. "It's funny, but you remind me of them in lots of ways."

"What ways?" Tyler said, and told himself it really didn't matter. Even if he shared the blood of the Baron brothers, he wasn't one of them. "What ways?" he asked again, and cursed himself for wanting to hear the answer.

"Well, Gage built his own empire, from the ground up." Caitlin lifted Tyler's hand, brought it to her lips. "I get the feeling you did, too."

He shrugged. "Working up a sweat doesn't mean much." He paused, cleared his throat. "What about the other two? What are they like?"

"Travis—he's the eldest—Travis is like you, too." She turned his hand over, kissed the callused palm. "He can go from being warm and charming to tough as steel in the blink of an eye. And Slade…" Caitlin smiled. "Let's just say that I'd love to see you and Slade play poker sometime. I don't know which of you would do a better job of calling the other's bluff.''

Travis nodded. "You, ah, you're fond of your stepbrothers," he said, after a moment.

"I adore them all." She sighed. "And I know you don't like hearing it, but I love Jonas, too." She felt Tyler stiffen and she turned and put her arms around his neck. "My mother married him when I was ten. Two years later, she ran off to New York with an actor she met at a little theater she'd conned Jonas into backing."

"And left you behind?" Tyler's mouth thinned. "Was the woman crazy?"

"Leaving me was the best thing she could have done, Tyler," Caitlin said, with a little smile. "By the time she married Jonas, I'd forgotten the names of half the men she'd lived with. Jonas kept me, even after he divorced her. He gave me a home. Stability. Love. Well, his kind of love, anyway."

"Love," Tyler said, and grimaced. "I've heard him talk to you, Cait. Does he ever do anything but bark?"

"That's just the way he is. It's not personal."

Tyler gave a bitter laugh. "Everything that SOB does is personal. I'll bet he thinks that sun rises just for his benefit."

"You see?" Caitlin smiled and brushed her mouth over his. "That's just what my brothers would say."

"Is it," he said, after a minute.

"You sound just like them. Even your voice has the same timbre." She smiled and touched the tip of her nose to his. "So?"

"So?"

"So, I've told you about me. Now I want to hear about you."

A muscle knotted in Tyler's jaw. "There's not much to tell."

Caitlin grinned. "Mr. Kincaid is the founder of Kincaid Incorporated," she said smugly, "which is based in Atlanta, Georgia. He serves on the board of several major corporations and he is honorary chairman of—"

To her absolute delight, Tyler blushed.

"Hell," he muttered, "you read that stupid brochure my PR department put out." He drew back, glared at her from under his brows. "How'd you get your hands on that?"

"Never underestimate a country girl, Mr. Kincaid." Caitlin laughed softly. "I turned on my computer, went out on the internet and looked you up."

He grinned. "Did you," he said softly.

"Yes. Yesterday. After you almost gave poor Leighton apoplexy with one look, I figured it might be a good idea to know just who I was up against, Kincaid."

She caught her breath as he slid his hands under the blanket and stroked them over her flesh.

"What a fine idea, McCord."

"Looking you up on the net?" she said, and shuddered as his fingers brushed over her breasts.

"Being up against me," he murmured, and cupped the back of her head. "Come here, McCord, and kiss me."

She did, and before her heart could take a second beat, the kiss went from soft and gentle to passionate and exciting.

"Tyler," she whispered.

"Cait." He turned her in his arms so she was facing him. The blanket slipped, unnoticed, from her shoulders. Sunlight bathed her skin with gold. Travis felt as if a fist were clenching around his heart. "Cait," he whispered, "take me inside you."

He watched her face change, watched her eyes darken, her mouth soften as he sought entrance. She smiled, a smile as old as Eve: "Yes," she sighed, "oh, yes."

Slowly, slowly, she impaled herself on his rigid length, taking him deep, filling herself with him, feeling her womb constrict as her soul took flight.

I love you, she thought, Tyler, I love you...but his mouth was on hers, his hands were on her hips, he was guiding her in this slow, lush dance, in steps her blood had always known.

And she lost herself in his embrace.

Afterward, he held her close while his breathing slowed and the earth steadied on its axis.

She was warm in his arms, as warm as a kitten basking in the sun, and just as pliant.

He stroked her hair and tried to make sense of what was happening to him.

He'd always been successful with women. There was no boastfulness in admitting it to himself. The simple fact was that there'd never been a woman he'd wanted that he hadn't been able to have.

But something else was happening here.

Each time he looked at Caitlin, each time he touched her, he felt... Tyler closed his eyes. That was the problem. He didn't know what he felt. It was as if something were stretching and stirring inside him.

And it scared the hell out of him..

He was thirty-five years old. He'd built an empire with nothing but his own sweat and skill; he'd run the rapids on Alaska's wildest rivers. He'd skydived, skied mountains without trails and gone spelunking in caves that stretched for miles—and he was terrified of whatever it was his heart was trying to signal to him about a woman he'd only met a week ago.

A woman who was the stepdaughter of the man he was determined to destroy.

Tyler looked down at Caitlin, nestled so sweetly in his arms. He had to tell her the truth. Who he was. Why he'd come here.

What he was going to do.

His mouth thinned.

God, he couldn't. It was too soon. How could he lay his life out to her that way? "I'm not Tyler Kincaid," he'd say. "I'm a man named John Smith. My mother is dead, my father is Jonas Baron but he refuses to admit it, and when I was younger, I did some things..."

His throat closed.

He'd never told those things to anyone. Those things had happened to John Smith. He was Tyler Kincaid. How could he even consider dumping all that on Caitlin? They'd only known each other for a short while, been lovers for a night.

And yet—and yet, if miracles were real, if magic could happen, if she felt what he felt...

"Tyler?"

He smiled, gathered her close as she sighed and stirred in his arms.

"Yes, love."

"Tyler." Her breath whispered against his throat; she kissed his damp skin, tasted it with the tip of her tongue. "I just wanted to say your name."

Tell her, he thought fiercely, tell her it's a name you created...

"And—and to tell you that I've never—I've never been so happy." She gave a little laugh and tilted her head back, so she could see his face. "If I had any feminine wiles at all, I'd know better than to tell you that."

He bent his head, caught her mouth with his and kissed her. "Cait," he murmured.

"I like it when you call me that. No one ever has." She smiled against his lips. "You know how I feel, Tyler?"

"As if your life is just beginning," he said, sliding his thumbs along her cheekbones. "As if this dawn is the start of the rest of your life."

"Yes! Yes, that's right. Oh, Tyler, I want—I want—"

"I know you do." Tyler framed her face with his hands. "But first, sweet Cait, I have things to tell you."

"Me, too." She sat up in his lap, her eyes glowing. "Something wonderful happened last night."

Tyler chuckled. "It certainly did."

Caitlin laughed and put her hands on his shoulders. "I mean, before I got here. Jonas called me into the library. He said he had something to tell me. That's when he told me you were going away."

"Now the woman admits it," he said softly, teasingly, filling his soul with the sight of her. "The old man told you I was leaving, and that made you happy?"

"Hush." She kissed him again, sat back and gave him a worried look. "Don't even joke about it. That part almost tore my heart out."

Tyler took a deep breath. "That's what I need to tell you, Cait. About why I came to Espada—and why I'm not leaving."

"You don't have to explain."

"I don't?"

"No, of course not. You bought a home here. You wouldn't have done that if you didn't intend to stay in Texas. And no matter what Jonas pretends, I know you're not the sort of man who'd knuckle under to his bullying." Caitlin moistened her lips. "I don't know what the trouble is between you, but I do know you won't run away from it."

Tyler linked his hands together at the base of her spine.

"That's right, Cait. I won't. I can't. I have business to settle with Jonas Baron, and until I do, I'm not going anywhere. Sweetheart, I know you think he's been good to you. Well, maybe he has, in his own selfish way, although how you can still believe it after he's told you, bluntly, that you're, hell, I don't know, less valuable to him because you don't carry Baron blood—"

"That's what I have to tell you. That's all changed."

"Changed?" Tyler repeated. "How has it changed?"

But he knew. Even before Caitlin said the words, he knew.

"Jonas changed his mind. He's decided to will Espada to me."

CHAPTER ELEVEN

FOUR days.

Four days had gone by since she'd spent the night in Tyler's arms.

Caitlin knew how much time had elapsed not only to the hour but to the minute, just as she knew how many times she'd thought about Tyler, wanted him, longed for him.

Now, she was starting to know how much she hated him.

Her mouth trembled as she led the mare from the stable. It was the same horse she'd been riding the day she'd almost run Tyler down. If only she hadn't gone riding that day. If only she'd ridden toward the hills, not toward the road.

Caitlin gave herself a shake. What was that old expression about not crying over spilled milk? You couldn't change the past. The future was what mattered, and her future was going to be wonderful.

Espada would be hers.

The mare whinnied and tossed her head.

"Easy, girl," Caitlin said softly, as she lay the saddle on the animal's back.

She'd always loved the quiet of early morning down at the stables. The grass, still wet with dew; the sun, warm on her face...all the creatures that called Espada home were stirring and stretching as the new day began.

Less than a week ago, she'd stirred and stretched in Tyler's arms. She'd greeted the dawn of another day with his kisses on her lips, his hands on her skin...

The mare snorted and danced sideways.

"Sorry," Caitlin murmured, and let out the cinch strap.

Thinking about that night, and that morning, was pointless. They'd happened and now they were over. And the sooner she stopped wondering why Tyler was doing this to her, the better.

"Mornin', Jonas."

She looked up. Jonas had joined Abel at the corral. His smile was almost as broad as the brim of his Stetson.

Her stepfather had been doing a lot of smiling lately, although he certainly hadn't been smiling when she'd returned to Espada on Sunday. She'd made the drive more on instinct than anything else, her heart filled with Tyler, her body still singing with their commingled passion. The world had seemed perfect—until she'd spotted Jonas, sitting on the front steps of the house, an unlit cigar clamped between his teeth and a scowl as dark as a thundercloud on his face.

She'd killed the engine, stepped down from the cab of her pickup truck and hesitated. She'd told herself not to be a fool. She was a grown woman, and if she wanted to stay out all night with a man Jonas didn't like, that was her business.

So she'd shut the truck door, squared her shoulders and walked briskly toward the house.

"Good morning," she'd said, and started past him, but Jonas had risen to his feet and blocked her passage.

"You know what time it is, missy?"

"Ten," she answered pleasantly, after a glance at her watch. "And I promised Abel I'd help him with the new stud, so if you'll excuse me—"

"Looks to me as if you've already been dealin' with the new stud."

Caitlin felt her cheeks burn, but her gaze was unflinching as it met her stepfather's.

"Don't," she said softly. "Please, don't say anything we'll both regret."

"I ain't sayin' nothin' but the truth. You been with Kincaid."

"Yes. I was with Tyler. And it has nothing to do with you."

Jonas spat the cigar into the grass. "It has everythin' to do with me, girl, and with Espada. I've been tryin' to tell you, Kincaid is no good. He come here after somethin' that ain't his to take."

"It's me he wants," she'd said softly. "Me, Jonas. Is that so difficult for you to accept?"

"You tell him I've decided to will Espada to you?"

The unease that had scrabbled at the edges of her mind during the drive home reached out for her, but she forced it aside.

"Believe it or not, Espada was hardly on our agenda."

Jonas grasped her arm. "Answer me, girl. Did you tell him?"

"Yes."

"And? What'd he say?"

Nothing. That was what Tyler had said. He'd simply looked at her, his face expressionless. Then he'd lifted her from his lap, set her on her feet and walked into the house.

"Tyler?" she'd said, staring after him, and he'd stopped, turned back, taken her in his arms and kissed her.

"Sorry," he'd murmured, holding her close. After a minute, she'd felt his body harden and he'd made love to her again, not gently but hard and fast so that when it was over, she'd been clinging to him, her skin flushed and damp, her breathing rapid. "Cait," he'd whispered, "Cait, forgive me," and she'd taken his face in her hands and told him there was nothing to forgive, that it had been exciting, being taken that way.

Staring into her stepfather's pale, chilly eyes that Sunday morning, she'd forced herself not to think of anything but Tyler, didn't let herself dwell on why Tyler hadn't responded to her wonderful news about Espada, why he'd made love to her with such desperation...

Why he'd asked her to forgive him.

She'd looked Jonas in the eye and told him to mind his own damned business. Then she'd gone into the house, up to her room, and phoned Tyler...

Phoned him, and reached his answering machine, the same as she'd reached it twice more before she'd realized he didn't want to talk to her, didn't intend to return her calls or to see her again.

"Goin' ridin'?"

Caitlin looked up. Jonas was strolling toward her, smiling pleasantly.

"Uh-huh." She made the final adjustments to the mare's

saddle and swung up into it. "She needs a good workout. I figured I'd take her out for a while."

"Well, you be back by lunchtime, you hear?" Jonas grinned. "Got a surprise for you."

"I'll be back." She touched her heels to the animal's sides but before she could move out, her stepfather grabbed the bridle.

"Don't you want to know what it is?"

Caitlin forced a smile. "It wouldn't be a surprise, if I knew."

Jonas chuckled. "Spoken like a true Baron," he said, and let go of the bridle.

A true Baron, Caitlin thought, and clucked softly to the mare. Was that what she was now? She must be; only a true Baron could inherit Espada. She waited for the rush of pleasure that should have accompanied the realization but it wasn't there. She hadn't felt pleasure over anything, not in days, not since she'd let herself face the truth, that Tyler wasn't going to call, that all she'd been was a one-night stand, a woman he'd leched after and, once he'd gotten what he'd wanted, there'd be nothing more.

The mare was edgy. Hell, so was she.

"Okay," Caitlin said, and gave the animal its head.

The mare headed for the northern hills that rimmed Espada's lush grazing land at a trot. Caitlin touched her heels to the horse's flanks and urged it into a gallop. A hot wind slapped at her face, lifted the damp curls from her forehead and she blanked her mind to everything but the heat, the horse and the scents of the meadow.

After a while, she slowed the pace to a trot, then to a walk. Caitlin leaned forward, patted the mare's arched neck. She and Abel had discussed the animal last night and decided it was time she gave Espada a foal.

"Pretty soon now," Caitlin said softly, " I'm going to introduce you to that handsome stud in the last stall." The mare's ears twitched. "Just take my advice, girl. Enjoy yourself—but don't believe a thing he says."

The mare whinnied and Caitlin laughed, but the laugh

caught in her throat and became a sob. She threw back her head and glared at the cloudless sky.

"Damn you to hell, Tyler Kincaid," she said. "Damn you to hell, forever."

Then she leaned forward, tightened her grasp on the reins and set the animal into a hard, fast gallop.

Tyler stood on the patio of his house in the Texas hills and stared out across the land.

An Express Delivery box had arrived that morning. It lay on the table behind him. He'd emptied it and now everything he'd spent a lifetime searching for lay neatly stacked inside his briefcase.

"I have everything you'll need, sir," the P.I. had told him when he'd called.

He sure as hell did.

There was a sworn statement from the woman who'd served as receptionist to the doctor who'd delivered a live male infant to Juanita Baron on July 18, thirty-five years before. Another from the doctor's wife, who'd listened to her husband's deathbed, guilt-ridden confession of his complicity in reporting the supposed stillbirth of that same infant boy.

And there was the most damning bit of evidence of all.

There, in that neat pile of papers, were documents that bore the name of the drifter who'd come onto the Baron ranch and into Juanita's life, all those years ago. There was little doubt he'd been her friend, her confidant...but not the father of her child. The private investigator had not only found the drifter's name, but he'd also found his history. The man had been in the army. He'd had medical records...

Medical records that made it clear the drifter could never have fathered a child. He'd suffered a hideous wound, while serving in the army—a wound that had, without question, left him sterile.

There was no doubt about it now. DNA tests, blood tests, Tyler would demand all of it, but the results would only confirm the truth.

Jonas Baron was his father.

Tyler swung away from the placid meadow and the rolling hills.

"Damn you to hell, you son of a bitch," he shouted, but the angry imprecation did nothing to relieve the pain and rage inside him. He pounded his fist on the glass-topped patio table but the glass was tempered and wouldn't break. And he wanted it to break, wanted to see it break, shatter into a thousand pieces, the way his life had been shattered.

And his heart.

If only he'd never begun this damned stupid quest for closure. If only he'd accepted Adrianna's birthday gift. If only he'd accepted his life. Most men would have been pleased with what he'd accomplished. The wealth. The power. The name people respected, and what did it matter if he'd created his name himself? He was Tyler Kincaid. The boy named John Smith was long-gone.

Except, there'd never been a John Smith. There'd been a boy born to Jonas and Juanita Baron, and the boy's mother had died knowing his father intended to abandon him.

Tyler picked up his briefcase, walked down the patio steps and across the grass.

A couple of weeks ago, the investigator's report would have had him cheering. He'd have had all the answers he needed, all the proof he wanted before he took his revenge on Jonas Baron.

And then he'd fallen in love with Caitlin.

What sense was there in denying the truth? He loved her, and once he did what he'd come here to do, she would hate him. He was going to destroy the stepfather she loved, make enemies of the brothers she adored and he'd never known, and strip her of the thing that was as much a part of her as her soul.

Espada.

"Jonas is willing Espada to me," she'd told him, and when he'd looked into her eyes, he'd known she was telling him something she thought wonderful.

Tyler stood still, his arms at his sides, his head bowed.

They said a drowning man's life flashed before his eyes but

he knew now that you didn't have to feel your lungs filling with water for that to happen. The old man was naming her the heir to Espada, she'd said, and Tyler had seen a score of images blaze to life inside his head. Himself, the night of his birthday party. The private investigator, when he'd promised to get all the facts. Jonas, boasting of how he'd tormented his first wife by telling her he'd give her child away. Caitlin, oh, Caitlin, her lovely face taut with passion as he took her virginity.

And, at the last, he'd seen the face of a woman he'd never known, a woman who'd given her life for his.

How could he abandon Juanita Baron? How could he dismiss her sacrifice and walk away? Closure? Closure didn't matter anymore. He'd come looking for some sordid little tale about a girl who'd gotten herself knocked up but he'd found a story that might have come out of the old Greek tragedies. A despairing wife. A cruel husband. A child whose first breath was taken as his mother's last breath left her body...

"Oh, God," Tyler whispered, lifting his face to the sky.

If he took Espada, he would break Caitlin's heart.

If he didn't, he'd never be able to live with the knowledge that he'd failed the woman who'd given him life.

He turned and stared blindly back at the house, at the patio where he'd held Caitlin in his arms and made love to her.

If only he'd told her everything that morning. The truth about himself. About his past, as ugly as it was. About what he intended to do. What he had to do. Most of all, most of all, he should have told her that he loved her.

She loved him, too. He knew it. Her love for him had shone in her eyes. Her kisses had tasted of it.

All right. She loved Espada. But maybe—maybe, she loved him more.

Tyler drew a deep breath, then let it out.

He'd sat in the dark, listening to her sweet voice on his answering machine. That first message, bright and joyful. The second, less certain but still loving. And the last message, when she'd said she'd understand if he didn't return her call...

Hell, no. She didn't understand. How could she? And how could he simply turn his back and walk away from her?

"I love you, Cait," he whispered.

The words seemed foreign as he spoke them. He'd never said them to another woman. Hell, he'd never said them to another human being.

She did love him. She did. He was sure of it. Okay. Okay, he thought, as he ran his hands through his hair, he wasn't sure. How could he be, when he'd never let her say the words, never said them to her?

It wasn't too late. But it was risky.

What if he was wrong? If she didn't love him? If what he'd seen glowing in her face was just the joy of a woman sexually fulfilled?

Tyler swallowed hard. He'd never know, unless he asked. Unless he took the risk. Dammit, he'd spent his life risking his neck, risking his wealth and his corporations. Admitting his love for Caitlin, counting on her love for him being its equal, would be the greatest risk he'd ever taken. If he was wrong...

If he was wrong, he'd lose her. But he'd lose her anyway, if he did nothing. And if he was right and she loved him, if she'd stand by him, once she knew the truth...

Tyler jumped into his truck, put it in gear and took it to its top speed in nothing flat.

Marta flung open the door as Caitlin came up the steps.

"There you are," she said, and put an arm around her step-daughter's shoulders. "We held lunch for you."

Caitlin smiled. "You shouldn't have bothered. Actually I'm not even hungry."

"Actually," a deep voice said, "you're as skinny as a bean-pole, sugar."

Caitlin squealed with delight and launched herself into Slade Baron's arms. "Slade," she laughed. "Slade, what a wonderful surprise."

"You just turn around, darlin', if you want to feast your eyes on a really wonderful surprise."

Caitlin spun out of Slade's arms. "Travis?"

"You bet," Travis Baron said, grinning as he opened his arms to his stepsister.

"Listen here, babe. You want the best surprise of all? Just take a gander at me."

Caitlin clapped her hand to her heart. "Gage," she said, and flung her arms around the neck of her youngest brother. "Gage, I can't believe it!"

Jonas, standing behind his three sons, gave a gravelly laugh. "Didn't I tell you I had somethin' special for you, missy?"

"Yes, but I never dreamed…" Caitlin smiled, kissed Travis again, grabbed hold of Gage and Slade and led them into the library as Marta made a discreet exit. "What are you guys doing here? How'd you all manage to get away at the same time? Where are Alexandra, and Natalie, and Lara? Gage, where's my gorgeous new niece? And Slade, where's my beautiful nephew? Travis, isn't Alex due any day now?"

The Barons all laughed. "That's our Catie," Gage said. "Always askin' a hundred questions in the time it would take most folks to ask one."

Caitlin sat down in the middle of a leather sofa. Slade took up residence in one corner, Travis in the other. Gage pulled the straight-back chair out from behind Jonas's desk, swung it around, straddled it and folded his arms along the top.

"Jes' make yourselves at home," Jonas said sarcastically.

His sons looked at each other. "Thanks," Slade said lazily. "We already have." He cleared his throat. "So, Catie darlin', how're you doin'?"

Not so good, she almost said, but caught herself in time. This unexpected visit was too wonderful to spoil and besides, her love life wasn't her stepbrothers' problem.

"I'm doing just fine." Her smile took in all three of them. "And you guys?"

"Oh, fine," Gage said.

Travis and Slade both nodded. "Fine," they said, in unison.

"And my wonderful sisters-in-law? My nephew? My niece?" She looked at Travis. "Do we get to know the sex of yours ahead of time, or what?"

He grinned. "Alex wants to do this the old-fashioned way. She told the doctor to keep the information to himself."

Caitlin laughed. "Good for her. Oh, I wish they'd all come with you. I wish…" She saw the three men glance at each other and the realization came, hard and fast. This wasn't just a visit, it was a meeting. She looked at Jonas. "Jonas? Is this about—is it about—"

"Espada." Jonas nodded as he opened a bottle of bourbon. "It sure is."

"Oh." Color rushed to her face. It was silly, but she suddenly felt flustered. "You told them?"

"I did."

She looked at the faces of the men she loved as much as if they really shared the same blood, hoping to read something in their expressions, but she couldn't.

"Guys, look, if any of you has changed his mind, if you want Espada, I'll understand. I mean, I'll be pleased, because you all certainly deserve the land more than I do—"

"Sugar," Slade said gently, "we couldn't be happier."

She nodded. "I'm glad, because I'd never want to take anything from any of you."

Gage reached out and took her hand. "We're happy for you, Catie."

Travis leaned over and kissed her cheek. "Damned right we are," he said gruffly, and shot a hard look at his father. "It's just too bad it took so long for our old man to come to his senses."

"Came to 'em, didn't I?" Jonas said. "That's what counts."

"Yeah," Slade said, "but only after you got jerked around by some no-account con man from Atlanta—"

"Slade," Travis and Gage both said, but it was too late.

"Hell," Slade mumbled. "I didn't mean… Catie, Sugar, I shouldn't have—"

"Tyler," Caitlin said, and wondered how she could sound so calm and cool when her heart was lifting into her throat. "You're talking about Tyler Kincaid."

"Well, go on," Jonas said. "Tell her."

Slade took a deep breath. "Yeah. We're talking about that
son of a bitch, Kincaid." He reached for her hand and clasped
it tightly in his. "The bastard took you in, Caitlin. I wish there
were some easier way to say it, but—"

"Took me in, how?"

Again, the sound of her own voice surprised her. Maybe it
was because whatever her brothers were about to tell her
would be no surprise. Oh, the details might be, but in her heart
she'd known all along that Tyler was too good to be true. That
such a strong, passionate, tender man should have come into
her life had to have been either a miracle or a mistake, and
she'd always known that life didn't deal in miracles.

"Took me in, how?" she repeated, as she took her hand
from Slade's and rose to her feet.

Her brothers looked at each other. Gage cleared his throat.
"He wants Espada."

"No." Caitlin looked from one unsmiling face to the other.
"No, you're wrong about that. He doesn't want—"

"He does." Travis cleared his throat, too. "Seems they
found oil in the west range. Lots of oil. It's gonna bring in a
lot of money."

"Jonas?" Caitlin turned to her stepfather. "Is that true?
How come you didn't tell me?"

"Only got the final reports a couple o' weeks ago," Jonas
said. "I didn't want to say nothin' till I was sure and by the
time I was, Kincaid was sniffin' around this place like a dog
after a lost bone."

"Sniffing around me, you mean," Caitlin said quietly. The
room was warm but her skin prickled as if a chill wind were
blowing. She wrapped her arms around herself and looked at
her brothers. "Jonas warned me. He said Tyler was after more
than me, but I wouldn't listen."

"Oh, darlin'," Travis said softly, and rose to his feet. "Catie—"

"No. No, I'm fine. Just tell me the rest. There's more, isn't
there?"

Gage stood up. "Nothing you need to hear, sweetheart.
Jonas says you've broken up with the bastard, so—"

"I haven't," she said, with her head held high. "He's broken up with me. And you're wrong, I do need to hear it. Tell me the rest."

Slade sighed and rose from the corner of the sofa. "The son of a bitch has a woman, back in Atlanta."

Caitlin couldn't help it. A soft moan slipped from her lips and she slapped both hands over her mouth, as if to keep in the cries that might follow it.

"A woman," she repeated quietly.

"Name of Aay-dreee-anna," Jonas said, drawing out the syllables as if the name were part of some complex, foreign tongue. "Jes' the type you'd figure him for. Looks like one of them models in a magazine."

"Beautiful," Caitlin whispered. "Sophisticated. Elegant."

Gage, Travis and Slade shared another look. We're going after Tyler Kincaid, the look said, and when we find him, we're going to beat the crap out of him.

"Phony as a three-dollar bill," Travis said coldly.

"All surface," Slade said, "no substance."

"They deserve each other," Gage added grimly, and the brothers nodded.

"You cannot believe the story the man made up," Jonas said. His sons and his stepdaughter looked at him and he shook his head and sighed. "Nobody would."

"You mean, that he was a drifter?" Caitlin said quietly. "Or—or that he was interested in me?"

"Catie," her brothers said, but Jonas's voice overrode theirs.

"You all know 'bout that grave up on the hill, that it's the restin' place of my first wife, who died in childbirth." He paused, looked at their faces and gave a deep sigh. "I loved that woman with all my heart. It damn near killed me, losin' her, along with my firstborn. It was a black day in my life. Now here we are, all these years later, a no-account liar named Tyler Kincaid comes walkin' onto my land. My land," Jonas said, thumping his chest, his voice rising, "and tells me he's gonna tell my kith an' kin a trumped up story of how my firstborn didn't die, a story that makes him out to be that child—''

"What?" Caitlin said. "What?"

"That's exactly what I said. I said, 'What are you talkin' about, Kincaid?' An' he laughed and said he'd found out about the oil on Espada, an' if I didn't sign the ranch over to him, he'd tell the world this ugly lie, that he'd drag the Baron name through the mud."

"But that's crazy." Caitlin looked at her stepfather. "He's Tyler Kincaid. He's got more money than he knows what to do with. He—"

"What he's got is the pedigree of a mongrel dog. He ain't nobody. Even the name 'Tyler Kincaid' is a lie."

"That's one hell of a performance, old man."

Everyone in the room turned around. Tyler stood in the doorway, dressed as Caitlin knew she'd always remember him, in a black T-shirt, faded jeans and boots, his hands on his hips and a look of contempt curled across his mouth.

"It's so good," he said, with a cold smile, "that I'm almost tempted to believe it myself."

"Git off my land, Kincaid," Jonas said. His three sons started forward with fury in their eyes but Caitlin ran past them, to Tyler.

"Tell me Jonas is wrong," she whispered. "Tyler?" She looked up at him, at the man to whom she'd given her heart. "Tell me he's wrong."

"He can't." Jonas's voice was cold. "Ain't that right, Kincaid? You can't tell her I'm wrong, cause I'm not."

Caitlin put her hand on Tyler's arm, felt the power of the tightly coiled muscles beneath his skin.

"Please, Tyler." Her voice broke. "Tell me it's all a lie. What Jonas said. About you claiming you're his son. About you not really being somebody named Tyler Kincaid..."

Tyler touched the back of his hand to her cheek. "I can't do that, Cait."

A sob ripped from Caitlin's throat. "I loved you," she said brokenly, "oh God, I loved you!"

"Cait," Tyler said urgently, "listen to me. Let me tell you the whole story."

"You've told our sister enough stories," one of the Barons said, but Tyler ignored him.

"Caitlin," he said, "I love you."

"He's lyin'," Jonas said.

"Did you hear me, Cait?" Tyler's voice was low and rough. "I love you. I've never said those words to another woman. Only to you."

Caitlin wanted to believe him. Oh, she wanted to believe that Tyler's kisses, his whispers, his caresses had been the truth, that he loved her as she loved him…

"Is there a woman waiting for you in Atlanta?" she said. "A woman named Adrianna?"

A muscle knotted in his jaw. "Yes. But it's not—"

Her hand whirred through the air and cracked against his cheek.

"Get out," she sobbed. "Get out, get out, get out!"

Tyler looked down into Caitlin's tear-stained face. Now was the time to tell her, to tell her brothers, everything. His briefcase was in his truck. All the proof he needed was inside it. All he had to do was get it and he'd destroy Jonas, wipe those looks of hatred from his sons' faces.

But the truth wouldn't take the emptiness from Caitlin's eyes. It wouldn't change the fact that he'd planned to gain Espada and destroy it. And, all at once, he knew that the things he'd come here for today—the destruction of Jonas Baron, vengeance for himself and for the woman who'd borne him—were insignificant.

The only thing that mattered, that could change his life, was the love he'd found in Caitlin McCord's arms.

"Cait," he said, his eyes only for her, "Cait, if you ever loved me, then love me now. Trust me. Give me your hand and come with me."

He almost thought she was going to do it. He saw, just for a second, the love shining in her tear-studded eyes, just as he'd seen it the last time he'd held her in his arms. But then her brothers stepped forward and surrounded her. Travis stood to her left, Slade to her right. Gage took up position behind her and put his hand on Caitlin's shoulder. She lifted her hand and lay it over Gage's.

"Cait?" Tyler said.

The look on her face was all the answer he needed.

He turned, a man whose heart had been ripped from his chest, and walked from the house and down the steps. He reached his truck, opened the door...and stopped. No. Hell, no. He wasn't going to let it end like this. He loved Caitlin. She loved him. He was going back into that house and if he had to fight all three of her brothers, he'd do it. He'd do whatever he had to do to get her alone, to make her listen.

He'd taken Caitlin McCord out of this house by force once before and, by God, he'd do it again.

Tyler swung away from the truck, started back to the house...and the front door opened.

"Tyler," Caitlin cried, "Tyler, wait."

A smile lit his face as she flew down the steps toward him. "Cait," he said, and caught her in his arms. "Cait, sweetheart..."

Her brothers ran out the door. "Kincaid, you son of a bitch," one of them yelled.

Tyler could feel the adrenaline pumping. He pushed Caitlin behind him and stood ready to take the Barons on. Suddenly Jonas pushed past his sons.

"Caitlin," he roared, "Caitlin, you get back here..."

The old man clutched his chest and teetered at the top of the steps. Then he tumbled down them, hit the ground and lay still.

CHAPTER TWELVE

THE hospital was big and modern. It had a brand-new cardiac care wing that had been built with the money of half a dozen oil-and-cattle rich Texans. Each benefactor had some part of the wing named for him. A small atrium. A patient library. A roof garden. A chapel.

The waiting room had been named for Jonas. Tyler wondered at the irony of the Barons gathering in a room named for the clan's head as they waited to hear if the old man was going to live or die. The greater irony was that he should be seated among them. He didn't give a damn what happened to Jonas. And he knew Jonas's sons would rather have had a rattlesnake in their midst than him, but none of that mattered.

Caitlin wanted him here. That was all he cared about.

He'd stood back as Jonas's sons, his wife and stepdaughter knelt beside the old man after he'd fallen. He'd kept his distance when the ambulance came and Jonas was taken away. Marta had ridden with her husband. Caitlin's brothers had climbed into one car and called out to her but she'd taken Tyler's hand, her face white and stricken.

"Stay with me," she'd pleaded, and after that, the hounds of hell couldn't have kept him from her side.

Her brothers had started to object but they must have seen something in his face because one of them said this was a stupid time to stand around and argue. A short while later, they'd all crowded into the waiting room. Not that the room was small. On the contrary. It was handsome and expansive, but the place seemed packed, just the same.

Tyler figured it had to do with all the emotions hanging in the air.

Marta sat in a corner of a long beige sofa. Her shoulders

were straight, her expression calm, but her hands trembled when Gage handed her a cup of coffee.

Caitlin was with Marta, holding her hand, talking quietly to her. Every once in a while she looked up and her eyes sought Tyler's, as if to be sure he was still there.

Yes, his eyes said in return, I'm here, Cait. I'll always be here, as long as you want me.

Slade, Travis and Gage looked at him occasionally, too. Their faces were taut with anger and he knew it wasn't because of anything they thought he'd done to Jonas; it was because they believed he'd hurt their stepsister. He knew it was crazy, that all three of them would try to beat him senseless first chance they got and that he'd undoubtedly take at least two of them with him before he went down, but he liked them.

How could he not like men who loved Caitlin so deeply?

Looking at them gave him an eerie feeling. They were his brothers. Well, his half brothers. They carried his blood, just as he carried theirs. He could see bits of himself in them, too. Travis's green eyes. Slade's dark hair. The shape of Gage's nose and even the way he walked...

And none of them would ever know it.

He wasn't going to tell the Barons who he was. What for? Jonas was old and broken, perhaps dying. Only a coward would see any sense in inflicting pain on a broken man. The truth would only fall like a yoke on the necks of the old man's wife and sons. No. No, there was no reason or purpose in inflicting pain on innocent people.

Tyler jammed his hands into his pockets and looked out the window.

Someday, he might tell Caitlin, but only because he didn't want any lies between them. There was no need to tell her now. Let her keep her memories of her stepfather. Let her inherit the ranch she loved without his doing anything to sully the process. He knew he'd have to tell her something but he'd come up with an explanation that would explain why he'd come to Espada in the first place, something she'd accept in lieu of Jonas's poisonous lies.

"Mrs. Baron?"

Tyler turned around. The doctor had entered the room. Marta and Caitlin had risen to their feet and stood facing him; Gage, Travis and Slade gathered around the women.

Tyler stayed where he was.

"Mrs. Baron... Marta." Esteban O'Connor took her hand. "Jonas had a heart attack."

Marta nodded. "Is he—will he survive?"

"Yes, I think so. It was a mild attack, and your husband is a strong man." O'Connor cleared his throat. "But he fractured his leg when he fell, and severed a blood vessel. We've stopped the bleeding but he's going to need a transfusion."

"Well, give him one, man," Gage said impatiently.

"We will. The lab's searching our rare blood donor list right now."

Slade frowned. "Your what?"

"Jonas needs blood from a special donor. He has a rare blood type. He had surgery before, years ago, and a transfusion."

"His gallbladder," Marta said.

"Yes. The transfusion saved his life, but because he has a rare blood type, he received an incompatible transfusion and made an anti-k antibody..." O'Connor shook his head. "Look, it's complicated. The bottom line is, Jonas needs blood from a donor who is negative for the k antigen."

The brothers looked at each other. "Well," Travis said, after a minute, "don't those things run in families?" He held out his arm, as if there were a needle and a technician waiting. "You got all three of Jonas Baron's sons standin' right in front of you, Steve. Just take what you need."

"I wish it were that simple, but it takes twenty-four hours to run the tests to check for the antigen and to test the safety of the blood."

"I have the blood you need, Doctor." The little group stared at Tyler as he walked slowly toward them. "My name is Tyler Kincaid. I've been a blood donor for years, and they typed me as being k antigen negative."

O'Connor grinned. "Son of a gun. You'll be on our rare blood list."

"I know I am."

Slade cleared his throat. "Steve? I thought you just said— I thought you said this k negative stuff is rare."

"It is. Only three people out of a thousand are k antigen negative."

The room fell silent. Tyler hesitated, but he knew it was time for the truth. "Jonas Baron is my father," he said quietly.

"It's a lie," Gage said, but Slade motioned him to silence.

"It's the truth." Tyler gave a bitter laugh. "Believe me, I'm no happier about it than you are." He turned to Caitlin. "I didn't know it, when I came here," he said softly. "I only knew that I'd been born on Espada. Then I learned I was Jonas's son. And when I did, I was determined to destroy him."

Caitlin jerked back, as if he'd struck her. "By seducing me," she whispered, and Tyler wanted to take her in his arms, tell her she was wrong, that he loved her, that what had happened between them had nothing to do with vengeance...

But the doctor was already asking him questions, drawing him aside, clapping him on the back and telling the stunned little group gathered around him that patients like Jonas owed their lives to voluntary blood donors like Tyler.

"It's the gift of life," O'Connor said, and Tyler wondered if only he saw the bitter irony in those words.

By the time he broke free and turned around, Caitlin was gone.

Everything went quickly after that.

They hustled Tyler away to be poked, prodded and questioned. Finally, in a small, quiet room, he lay back and let a technician draw his blood. When she'd finished, she gave him a bright smile and slapped a gauze pad over the vein in his arm.

"There," she said briskly. "That's it, Mr. Baron."

"Kincaid," Tyler said. "My name is Tyler Kincaid."

The woman colored. "Of course. Sorry, Mr. Kincaid."

He nodded, did his best to make it look as if he was paying

attention to her instructions, but all he could think about was that he'd reached the end of his journey. He'd found his identity, found his brothers, found the only woman he'd ever love—and lost them all, the instant Jonas fell down those steps. By now, they all knew the whole truth. He'd tossed his keys to Travis, just before he'd headed down the hall with the doctor.

"There's a briefcase in my truck," he'd said. "You might as well know everything."

Tyler slipped from the examining table. The room spun a little; he shut his eyes, waited a couple of seconds, then opened them again.

It was over. His search for his identity, his quest for his roots—it was over, over and done with, and he wished to God he'd never embarked on it in the first place.

What had he learned, that could possibly make his life better? That his mother hadn't abandoned him? Well, yeah, that was good to know—but was it really better to know he'd been abandoned, instead, by his father? That his mother had died, knowing her baby was going to be given away?

She'd died thirty-five years ago. A lifetime ago, and nothing he could do now, nothing he'd intended to do now, could change that.

Tyler walked down the silent hospital corridor.

He'd come to Texas determined to find answers, and he'd found them…but he'd found something else, too, something he'd never even known he was looking for.

And he'd lost it.

His footsteps slowed. They were still in the waiting room, the Barons and Caitlin. He paused just outside the doors. He could see them, all of them. The perfect family. Marta was seated on the couch again, smiling up at Travis and Gage and Slade. Caitlin was sitting beside her but suddenly she looked up and saw him…

Looked at him as if he were a stranger, then turned away.

Tyler began walking. His steps quickened, his shoulders straightened. What in hell was the matter with him? He hadn't lost anything. He hadn't found anything, either, except an old man who didn't want him any more today than he had thirty-five years ago. As for love... Love? He laughed as he stepped out into the heat of the afternoon. What was love, anyway? A man saw a woman he wanted, he played the game, said the right things, hung around and, eventually, he took her to bed. That was exactly what he'd done with Caitlin.

If it weren't for the stress of the last couple of weeks, he'd never have deluded himself into thinking he felt anything more than desire for her. If he ever loved a woman, it would be someone like Adrianna. Someone sophisticated. Urbane. Someone who knew the real Tyler Kincaid, the man in the Armani suits, not the guy in jeans and T-shirts and boots.

Not the guy who'd once sat watching the sun rise over the gentle Texas hills, while he held a soft, sweet woman in his arms.

Tyler cursed, climbed into his truck, threw it into gear and shot away.

His home in Atlanta was just as he'd left it. The marble foyer gleamed; the chandelier glittered. There was a stack of mail on the hall table and he sorted through it but none of it seemed important, and after a couple of minutes, he tossed it aside.

There were only a few messages on his answering machine. He'd checked it while he was away so he didn't expect much that was urgent to be on it now. He was right. There wasn't. The only message he listened to, in its entirety, was from Adrianna.

"Darling," she said in her soft, upper-class drawl, "I called your office and your secretary told me you were away. Now I understand why you haven't phoned. You must be terribly busy, but do get in touch, when you have a minute. You missed the Forsythe's party but there's one coming up at the Hutchinsons' that sounds like fun."

Tyler went into his kitchen, took a bottle of ale from the refrigerator, opened it and went back into his study. He hit the replay button and listened to Adrianna's message again while he tilted the bottle to his lips.

She wasn't just beautiful and bright, she was clever. She

knew how to handle a man. He hadn't called her in almost
three weeks but you'd never know it. She'd managed to make
it sound as if there were a perfectly reasonable explanation for
his silence.

Caitlin would probably have marched up to his door and
demanded to know if he was deliberately trying to avoid her.
Caitlin would...

Tyler frowned.

What did it matter what Caitlin would do? She wasn't in
his life anymore. She'd never been in his life, not in the life
that mattered. Even trying to imagine her here, in this house,
in his circle of friends, was laughable.

He was Tyler Kincaid. He didn't belong on a Texas ranch,
with manure on his boots and dust on his jeans. He belonged
here, in a world he knew. A world he'd created, with his own
two hands. And Adrianna fit into that world, perfectly.

Tyler picked up the telephone. Adrianna was right for him.
Or someone like Adrianna. A woman he could think about
when he was with her, not think about when he wasn't. One
who'd never intrude, get into his head when he didn't want
her there. One who wouldn't expect him to carry her, naked,
into the dawn of a new day; who wouldn't look at him with
her heart and her soul visible in her eyes...

"Dammit," he said, and slammed down the phone.

He was tired. Of course he was tired. He'd driven from
Texas to Atlanta, done it damned near straight through with
only a couple of bathroom breaks and endless cups of strong,
black coffee.

Tomorrow, he thought as he went up the stairs, tomorrow,
he'd phone Adrianna. He'd phone his vice president and his
secretary, tell them he was back and that things were returning
to normal. Better than normal. That deal in Stockholm was
probably still on the table. He'd tell his people to set up a
meeting, fly to Sweden, make an offer.

Maybe he'd take Adrianna with him. Maybe not. Tyler
smiled as he stripped off his clothes and stepped into the
shower. Scandinavian women were spectacularly beautiful.
Blond hair. Blue eyes. Just what he needed, just the thing to

stop him wondering, as he had from the start, if Caitlin's eyes were gold or brown or green, and how her hair could look like autumn and feel like silk as it drifted over his naked skin...

His mouth thinned.

"Stop it," he said sharply.

He finished showering, fell into bed...and dreamed of sunrises and soft sighs when he finally managed to fall asleep. He awoke before dawn and worked out in his private gym until his mind felt clear. Then he showered, phoned his office—and Adrianna.

By five o'clock, he'd held three meetings, spoken with Stockholm, lunched with his broker and talked with his travel agent about spending a few days in Sweden. By six, he'd showered and shaved in his private bathroom, changed into a tux and climbed into his Porsche for the trip to Adrianna's apartment.

"Tyler, darling," she said when she opened the door, and she went into his arms. He knew, as he held her, that she didn't really want to go to the Hutchinsons' party, that what she wanted was for him to strip her out of her black silk gown and out of the black lace garter belt and bra she was probably wearing underneath. His hands went to the zipper at the back of the gown, and all at once he thought of sundresses the colors of flowers, of scraps of white lace, and his hands stilled.

"We don't want to be late," he said lightly.

By seven, he was drinking vintage champagne from Baccarat flutes and wondering how red wine in plastic glasses could have tasted better.

By eight, he was eating beef Wellington and wishing it were barbecue.

By nine, he knew it wasn't working.

His body was in Atlanta but his heart and soul were in Texas. And, dammit, if Caitlin McCord was too stubborn, too pigheaded, too just plain impossible to admit that she loved him the way he loved her because, by God, he *did* love her, he always would, and he was tired of pretending he didn't. If she wouldn't admit it, well, it was up to him to make her acknowledge the truth.

Some women could be wooed with candlelight and flowers. Some could be persuaded with soft lights and softer music, but he knew damned well none of that would work with Caitlin. A man had to take a tougher stand with a woman like her. He had to show her who was in charge…

Show her that she held his heart in her hands, that he couldn't live without her any more than she could live without him, and if he had to toss her over his shoulder and carry her off to do it, by God, he would.

He drew Adrianna into a quiet corner of the Hutchinsons' house and took both her hands in his.

"Adrianna," he said softly, "Adrianna, I'm sorry. You're a wonderful woman. A beautiful woman—"

"But you've found someone else."

"Yes," he said, because she deserved honesty. "I have. Believe me, Adrianna, I didn't intend for this to happen."

Adrianna smiled, cupped his face with her hands, rose on her toes and kissed his mouth gently.

"You're a fine man, Tyler Kincaid," she said softly. "You're the best man I've ever known."

"Am I?" he said, in surprise.

Tears glittered in her eyes. "You are. And I'm sure the lucky woman you've fallen in love with knows it, too."

Tyler smiled. "Thank you," he said, and kissed her mouth, as gently as she'd kissed his.

He moved quickly after that, as if every second were urgent. He drove home, put on his jeans and his T-shirt and his boots, drove to the airport and chartered a plane. The pilot raised his eyebrows when Tyler said he had to be in Texas before sunrise, but he said it was no problem.

They touched down on the Baron airfield at some hellish hour of the early morning. Tyler half expected Abel or one of the men to come stumbling out of the bunkhouse as he made his way toward the main house but nobody did.

He smiled grimly.

Maybe the Baron cowpokes were accustomed to people flying in at all hours but he was pretty sure they weren't accustomed to what came next.

He rang the doorbell, rang it again, then pounded on the door with his fist. Lights blazed on inside but Carmen got to the door first.

"Señor Kincaid?" She blinked blearily at him. "What is the matter, *señor?*"

"Nothing's the matter," Tyler said, and moved past her, into the foyer. "I've come for Caitlin McCord."

Marta came down the stairs, clutching a blue robe to her throat. "Mr. Kincaid?"

"Yes," Tyler said. "I'm sorry to barge in on you this way, Mrs. Baron." His voice softened. "I called the hospital. They told me Jonas—they said your husband will be fine."

"Thanks to you," Marta said, and smiled. "I'm so glad you came back, Tyler. May I call you Tyler?"

"Yes. Of course. But—"

"Come in, please. Carmen? Make us some breakfast, will you? And tell my stepsons and my stepdaughter that we have a guest."

"No need to bother," a raspy male voice said.

Tyler looked further up the staircase. Gage, Travis and Slade stood one behind the other on the steps. They all looked sleep-tousled, cold-eyed and eminently likable, and Tyler sighed and wished to hell he could at least get to know them before he took them on.

"No need to bother, is right," an angry female voice said, and his heart turned over.

"Hello, Cait," he said softly, as the woman he loved came striding down the stairs toward him.

She was wearing a long white nightgown sprigged with tiny blue flowers. Her feet were bare and peeped out from under the hem, and her hair spilled over her shoulders in a wild, glorious tangle.

"You turn around and get your tail out of here, Tyler Kincaid!"

Tyler smiled, leaned back against the doorjamb and folded his arms over his chest.

"Get yourself dressed, McCord," he said calmly.

"You're a crazy man, Kincaid. Do you hear me? A crazy man, if you think I'm going to take orders from you."

Tyler lifted his hand, looked at his watch. "I'll give you three minutes."

"*You'll* give *me* three minutes?" Caitlin tossed her head and laughed. "Funny as well as crazy, Kincaid." She stopped laughing, folded her arms in an unconscious imitation of him, and fixed him with an angry glare. "How about giving me one good reason why you think you can walk in here and order me around?"

"Well," he said lazily, as he stepped away from the door and started toward the stairs, "well, McCord, actually, I could give you several, starting with the fact that it's almost dawn and I want us to get to my ranch in time to see the sun come up the way we did last time, both of us on my patio, naked as the day we were born."

He saw a blur of motion out of the corner of his eye, saw an arm shoot out in restraint and heard one of the brothers— one of *his* brothers, say, very softly, "Let's just wait a minute."

Caitlin's cheeks turned pink. "What a horrible man you are!"

"I could also tell you that if you don't get dressed and come with me willingly, I'm just going to have to toss you over my shoulder and carry you away."

"Kidnap me, you mean," Caitlin said furiously. "Did I tell you that, Gage? Travis? Slade? Did I tell you this man kidnapped me from this very house?"

Tyler mounted the steps slowly, his eyes never leaving hers. "I could give you all those reasons, McCord, but I won't." He stopped on the step below hers, so they were eye to eye, and he smiled. "I won't, because the only reason worth anything, the only one worth you hearing, is the simplest one of all." He reached out, clasped her face in his hands. She tried to jerk back but he could see the glitter of tears in her eyes, see something more that gave him hope. "I love you," he whispered. "I've loved you from the minute you tried to run me down with that horse."

"I did not try to run you down," Caitlin said. Her voice shook. Tears leaked from her eyes and, dammit, she just knew that her nose was going to start leaking, too, any second. "And you don't love me. You seduced me because you hated Jonas, and—"

Tyler kissed her. She told herself not to react, not to close her eyes or to let her mouth part to his, but the sweetness of his lips, the feel of his hands in her hair...

"I seduced you because I knew I couldn't live without making you mine," he whispered. "And I don't hate the old man. I thought I did but life is too short for hating." His eyes went to her mouth. "Hell, sweetheart, it's hardly long enough for loving. For the kind of loving I want us to share for the next hundred years, anyway."

Marta cleared her throat. "Well," she said briskly, "I think I'll, uh, I'll go get dressed. Carmen? Make breakfast, would you please? And boys..." She looked up the stairs, at her stepsons, and sighed. It was simple to see they weren't going anywhere. She sighed again as she made her way past them.

"You don't love me," Caitlin said. "You're only saying it because—because—"

Tyler arched a brow. "Because?"

"Because you want to hurt Jonas."

"Jonas hasn't got a damned thing to do with you and me, Cait. He never did."

"Well, then, you're saying it because you want Espada."

"Uh-huh." Tyler grinned. "So, let's see. I'm going to marry you so I can wait for you to inherit Espada—"

"Marry me?" Caitlin said. "Marry me? Never!"

"Marry you," Tyler said agreeably, "in, what? A week? A month?" He glanced up the stairs at Slade, Travis and Gage. "How long does it take to plan a wedding, anyway?"

"Five minutes," Travis said, "if you don't let the women take it out of your hands."

The brothers laughed, and Caitlin's face went from pink to purple.

"What is the matter with you three?" she hissed. "Get down here, pronto. Drag this man outside. Beat him up. Put him on the back of a horse and send him packing."

Tyler chuckled and kissed her again. He felt a tremor go through her, and his heart soared. But he wasn't about to let her know that, not yet. His Cait could be a tricky filly to handle.

"The days when the sheriff put a guy on the back of his horse and told him to get out of town before nightfall are gone, sweetheart. The time when a man controlled his wife's property is history, too." He slid his hands into her hair, tilted her face, her beautiful face, to his. "This is morning, Cait, the start of a new day. The start of our life, together. Espada will always belong to you. The Lazy S will belong to the both of us."

"The Lazy S?"

"Uh-huh." He kissed her again, taking longer this time, drinking in the sigh that trembled on her lips. "I'm naming the ranch I bought for the sunrise. Our sunrise. Is that okay with you?"

Caitlin swallowed hard. "Kincaid..."

"McCord."

"Kincaid, did you really think you could just—just show up here and—and sweet-talk your way back into my life?"

"Yes," he said simply. "I did. I love you, Cait. And you love me. And we're going to get married and have a houseful of kids, and every last one of them is gonna call Jonas Baron 'Grandpa.'"

Travis, Gage and Slade sent up a cheer. Tyler flashed them a grin and before she could move, scooped Caitlin off her feet and into his arms. She shrieked and looked at her stepbrothers.

"Are you just going to stand there and let him do this?" she said, trying to sound indignant and succeeding only in sounding breathless.

"I don't know," Gage said. He grinned as he watched her wrap her arms around Tyler's neck. "Are we, guys?"

"No way," Travis said solemnly. "For instance, I'm gonna

go open the door for our new brother. Seems like a man with an armful of woman can't be expected to do that for himself.''

"Good idea," Slade said, and dug in the pockets of his half-zipped jeans. "Tyler? You need wheels, bro?"

Tyler smiled. "Come to think of it, I guess I do."

"The blue pickup," Slade said, and tossed his keys.

"You're all impossible," Caitlin sputtered as Tyler carried her out the door and down the steps. "I swear, I'll get you for this. Slade? Gage? Travis? You hear me?"

"Yeah," Gage said gently. "We hear you, Catie. Loud and clear."

She did her best to glower over Tyler's shoulder because it was the right thing, but all she could manage was a smile filled with happiness.

"You put me down," she said, as he walked toward the blue pickup truck because that was the right thing, too, even though it was the last thing she wanted.

Tyler kissed her. "I will," he said, "just as soon as we get to that patio."

He put her in the passenger seat of the truck, buckled her in and got behind the wheel. She folded her arms, looked straight ahead and refused to say a word until they reached the house he'd bought in the hills.

"We're just in time," Tyler said, as he carried her across the dewy grass and onto the patio. "It's almost sunrise."

"As if that means a thing to me," Caitlin said. It was getting more and more difficult to sound angry. How could a woman sound angry, when her heart was racing with the wonder of knowing that all her dreams were coming true?

In the distance, the first hesitant blush of the morning sun was coloring the hills.

Tyler lowered her slowly to her feet. "I love you, Cait." He clasped her face in his hands and looked deep into her eyes. "And I need to hear you tell me that you love me, too."

"You're an impossible man, Tyler Kincaid. An absolutely impossible—"

"It's one of my finest qualities," he said humbly.

Caitlin laughed and, as she did, joyful tears rose in her eyes and glittered on her lashes.

"Oh, Tyler," she whispered. She lay her hands on his chest, rose on her toes and kissed his mouth. "I do love you. I adore you, and I always will."

His arms closed tightly around her. She was soft and warm and she smelled of flowers and sunshine, which was impossible considering that the sun was just beginning its climb into the sky, but Tyler had given up trying to understand anything beyond the fact that he loved Caitlin McCord more than any man had ever loved any woman, and that he would love her until they were both as old and crotchety as Jonas.

The thought made him chuckle.

"What?" Caitlin said, and leaned back in his arms.

"I was just thinking what a long and happy future we have stretching ahead of us, McCord."

"There you go, Kincaid. You're always so darned sure of yourself..." She caught her breath as he began undoing the tiny buttons down the front of her nightgown. "Whatever are you doing?"

"I'm making love with the woman I'm going to marry."

Caitlin smiled. "What an excellent idea," she whispered, and reached for his belt.

And, as the sun painted the Texas hills with flame, Tyler and Caitlin joined together in a love they knew would last forever.

EPILOGUE

SLADE BARON looked into the mirror in his old bedroom, tugged at the uneven ends of his formal bow tie and sighed as it came undone.

"It's a female conspiracy," he said, "that's what it is. Why in heck do women like to see men all gussied up in these monkey suits?"

Lara, his wife, smiled at his reflection.

"It's either because we know it drives you crazy or because we go weak in the knees at the sight of you looking so handsome," she said sweetly. "Turn around, and let me fix that for you."

Slade did as she'd asked. "Now, sugar, you know I look handsome no matter what I'm wearin'," he said, and grinned.

"Maybe," Lara said, trying her best not to smile, which wasn't easy, considering that her husband was gathering her close in his arms. "Slade Baron, I'm never going to get that tie fixed if you do that."

"Do what?" Slade asked innocently, and kissed her.

Lara sighed and lay her head against his shoulder. "I love you," she said softly.

"And a darned good thing you do," Slade said gruffly. He pressed a kiss into her hair. "I just hope Tyler and Caitlin can be half as happy as we are, sugar."

"Only half?" Lara asked, leaning back in his arms and smiling up at him.

"The way I figure it, nobody in the world could be this happy," Slade said, and drew his wife toward him for another kiss.

"Mommy? Daddy?"

Slade and Lara turned around. Their son, just awakened from his nap, stood clutching the bars of his Portacrib. Lara gave her husband a quick kiss, then went to scoop Michael into her arms.

"Hello, precious." She looked at Slade and smiled. "He's getting too big for that crib."

Slade held out his arms and took his son from her. "I know." He smoothed the child's dark curls and smiled back at his wife. "I do hate to see that crib put away, though."

Lara colored prettily. "Well, it won't be put away for long," she said, and lay a hand lightly over her flat belly.

Slade's gray eyes darkened. "Lara? Sugar, do you mean it?"

"Yes," she said softly, the love shining in her eyes. "I saw the doctor yesterday."

Slade's throat constricted. He wanted to tell his wife what she meant to him, that she had changed his life forever, but he couldn't speak. Instead he held out his arm and she went into his embrace, and he thought, as he held his son and his wife close to his heart, that he was the luckiest Baron who'd ever been born.

Travis came into his old bedroom quietly, shut the door and stood looking down at the big old armchair near the window. His wife, his beautiful wife, sat in it with their daughter in her arms. Alexandra had been nursing Amy. Now, the both of them had drifted off to sleep.

Travis's heart swelled with love. He was still trying to figure out what he'd done to deserve such happiness. All he knew for certain was that he was the luckiest Baron who'd ever been born.

Alexandra sighed and opened her eyes. She saw Travis and her face lit with joy.

"There you are," she said softly. "I missed you."

He smiled and knelt down beside his wife and child. "I was out on the deck," he said, and took Alex's hand, "talkin' with Tyler."

Alex grinned. "Telling him all about the horrors of married life, were you?"

"Yeah," Travis said, and grinned back at her, "somethin'

like that." His grin faded. "I can't stop thinkin' about how he grew up. The bad times he had, because of what the old man did."

Alex lifted her husband's hand to her mouth and kissed it. "It was a terrible thing, I know. Jonas, believing his first wife had taken a lover..."

"Jonas," Travis said tightly, "is Jonas. He's a stubborn old coot and he'll never change."

"Hush." Alex leaned forward and kissed her husband's mouth. "Tyler's forgiven him, darling. You have to, too."

"I know. It's just... I look at our baby and I wonder how anybody, even Jonas, could have abandoned a child."

"He made a terrible mistake, Travis. And he's doing his best to make up for it."

"Yeah." Travis smiled. "Anyway, Tyler and Catie found each other. That never would've happened, if Tyler hadn't come searchin' for the truth." He leaned forward, kissed his daughter's forehead, then kissed his wife's mouth. "I know the two of them can never be as happy as we are, darlin'. Nobody could be. But if they're half as much in love as you and me..."

"Half as much will be more than most people ever know," Alex whispered, and leaned forward again, for her husband's kiss.

Gage sat on the edge of the bed in his old bedroom and watched his beautiful wife and his precious daughter gaze solemnly into the mirror.

"You see?" Natalie said. "Jenny looks beautiful."

Jenny nodded and tucked her thumb into her mouth.

"And it would be *sooo* nice if Jenny could keep looking beautiful until after Aunt Catie and Uncle Tyler are married."

Jenny nodded again.

"You think she's got it?" Natalie said, looking at her husband in the mirror.

"Absolutely," Gage said, and tried not to laugh. If there was one thing he knew about his baby, it was that she couldn't keep clean, not even for a minute. She was the champion tod-

dler of them all, he thought proudly, and every inch of her
was a tomboy.

"I think so, too," Natalie said, and set her daughter gently
on the floor. She looked back into the mirror. "How do I
look?"

"Gorgeous," Gage said. He rose from the bed and went
toward her. "In fact," he whispered, and pressed a kiss to her
bare shoulder, "maybe we ought to pass on the wedding and
just stay up here and make out."

Natalie laughed, turned in her husband's arms and linked
her hands behind his neck. "I'll tell you what, Mr. Baron.
You behave yourself this afternoon and I'll ask Carmen if
she'll watch Jenny tonight." She gave him the sort of look
that turned his knees to rubber. "And then you can drive us
up to Superstition Butte and we'll, uh, we'll look at the stars."

"You got a deal, babe." Gage's smile faded as he looked
down into his wife's face. "Ah, Nat," he said softly, "I'm
the luckiest Baron who ever lived."

"And I'm the luckiest woman," Natalie said, and lifted her
mouth for his kiss.

Gage pressed his cheek to her hair. "Tyler and Caitlin really
love each other."

"Mmm. I know. Isn't it wonderful to see?"

"If they can only love each other half as much as we do,
babe, they'll be happy for the rest of their lives."

"For the rest of their lives," Natalie said dreamily, and then
she groaned. "Oh, Jenny..."

"What?" Gage said, and looked around.

Their little girl had found Natalie's lipstick. She was sitting
in the middle of the carpet, happily dabbing blobs of red all
over her pretty pink dress.

Natalie and Gage looked at her, then at each other, and they
laughed.

"You're going to be the hit of the party," Gage said, as he
scooped up his daughter. He put his other arm around his wife,
and wondered, not for the first time, what he'd ever done to
deserve such happiness.

*   *   *

At last, the moment had come.

Tyler thought he'd been ready but when he heard the first triumphant chords of Mendelssohn begin, when he looked up the flower-bedecked aisle that led from the garden to the waterfall decks of the Baron mansion and saw his bride start toward him on Jonas's arm, his heart threatened to stop beating.

Caitlin. His Caitlin. She was so beautiful in her ivory lace gown. And that look on her face, the way her eyes were fixed only on him...

"Just look at my Cait," he said softly.

His three brothers, standing alongside him, groaned softly.

"The man's a goner," Gage whispered.

"A pushover," Travis murmured.

"Just a fool for a purty face," Slade added.

All four brothers grinned at each other, and then Tyler's grin faded and he looked at his bride and wondered what he'd ever done in his life to be so damned lucky.

Caitlin's sisters-in-law, who were also standing under the flowered canopy at the altar, gave a communal sigh as they watched her come slowly up the aisle.

"Isn't she lovely?" Natalie whispered.

"Perfect," Alex said.

"Perfect," Lara echoed, and the three women sighed again.

The music swelled, just as Caitlin and her stepfather reached the altar. Jonas turned to Caitlin, lifted her bridal veil back from her face and cleared his throat

"You take good care of my girl," he said to Tyler, and stuck out his hand.

Tyler hesitated, but only for a second. Then he took his father's hand and shook it.

"You know that I will."

"And you, missy. You take good care of this man." Jonas cleared his throat again. "You take real good care of my son."

Caitlin smiled into Tyler's eyes. "For the rest of my life."

"Dear friends," the clergyman said, "we are gathered here today to join Tyler Kincaid and Caitlin McCord in marriage..."

Jonas stepped back beside Marta, who looped her arm through his.

"They're such a handsome couple," she said softly.

Jonas nodded. "They are that." He harrumphed. "Can't seem to get this frog outta my throat."

Marta leaned her head against his shoulder and smiled. "I know."

"Saw old Leighton, a while ago." Jonas chuckled. "Lady who did the flower arrangements seems to have her eye on him."

"And he's eyeing her, right back." Marta smiled again. "A good woman may be just what Leighton needs."

"A good woman's what every man needs," Jonas said, and covered his wife's hand with his. "Marta? You think Catie likes those pearls I gave her this mornin'?"

"She loves them. And they're magnificent. Just right, with her gown."

"Yeah." Jonas hesitated. "They belonged to Tyler's mother. To Juanita. I loved her, you know. You don't mind me tellin' you that, do you? It was so long ago…"

"No," Marta said gently, "I don't mind at all."

"If I could only go back and change things…" Jonas sighed. "I guess I never understood Juanita, or how to make her happy, but I know she'd want Catie to have those pearls."

"Did you tell that to Caitlin?"

"Yeah. I did. You, uh, you think she'll tell Tyler?"

"I'm sure she will. And I'm sure he'll be pleased."

"Yeah," Jonas said again, his voice gruff. "The thing of it is, I ain't always been the father I should have been, to any of my sons. But—but—" He turned to his wife, his pale eyes suspiciously bright. "It's not too late, is it?" he whispered. "To let 'em know I'm proud of 'em? That—that I'm pleased they turned into such fine men?"

"To tell them you love them, you mean."

Jonas nodded, and Marta took her husband's hand in hers.

"It's never too late for love," she said softly.

Jonas smiled and kissed her, and then they both joined in

the applause as Tyler and Caitlin shared their first kiss as husband and wife.

* * * * *

Acknowledgment

Many thanks to Dr. Mike Strong, who explained rare blood types, antibodies and antigens to me with clarity and patience. Thanks, as well, to donors everywhere, who unselfishly give the gift of life. Of course, any errors or omissions are solely mine.

If you enjoyed what you just read,
then we've got an offer you can't resist!

Take 2 bestselling
love stories FREE!
Plus get a FREE surprise gift!